"Here. It's not

Matt didn't need a
hadn't expected a
the thick slice of ch
of muscle but never turned his nose up at a free
dessert.

"Thank you. Cherry is my favorite."

"I'm glad." She opened her door. "Well, thank you again. Good night, Mr. Taylor."

"Good night, Mrs. McGuire. Ms.? Miss?"

There was a drawn look to her features that spoke of fatigue. "I'm divorced. Corie will do just fine."

"Matt will do, too. For me. I'm Matt. Not married. Never have been."

She smiled in that way that made him feel like he hadn't just stuck his foot in his mouth and made an awkward conversation downright uncomfortable. "Good to know. Good night, Matt."

He waited in the hallway, hearing the dead bolt, a chain and the doorknob engage. Good. He liked that she was cautious about her safety.

Once he got home, Matt didn't even bother grabbing a fork. He picked the wedge up in his hand and took a bite. A second bite made him forget the niggling thought at the back of his mind that told him something was very wrong in that small apartment across the hall.

There was also something very right about that little family.

DEAD MAN DISTRICT

USA TODAY Bestselling Author
JULIE MILLER

⟨H⟩ HARLEQUIN
INTRIGUE

For the Grand Island Book Club, who so graciously took me to
dinner and talked about my book! I was honored, and I had fun.
Lindsey, Micki, Jessica, Jodi, Mary, Jana, Kristen—you are all
fabulous, intelligent, accomplished young women and
terrific moms, and I thank you.

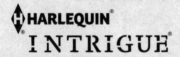

Recycling programs
for this product may
not exist in your area.

ISBN-13: 978-1-335-40150-2

Dead Man District

Copyright © 2020 by Julie Miller

Harlequin Enterprises ULC
22 Adelaide St. West, 40th Floor
Toronto, Ontario M5H 4E3, Canada
www.Harlequin.com

Printed in U.S.A.

Julie Miller is an award-winning *USA TODAY* bestselling author of breathtaking romantic suspense—with a National Readers' Choice Award and a Daphne du Maurier Award, among other prizes. She has also earned an *RT Book Reviews* Career Achievement Award. For a complete list of her books, monthly newsletter and more, go to juliemiller.org.

Visit the Author Profile page at Harlequin.com.

CAST OF CHARACTERS

Matt Taylor—A KCFD firefighter. He's big, he's tough, and he saves lives. But can he win the most important battle of his life—saving the family next door?

Corie McGuire—There's no mistaking this single mom is falling for the quiet, sexy firefighter who lives across the hall. Keeping her son safe is job one. She'll turn to Matt for protection. But does she dare give him her heart?

Evan McGuire—Corie's sensitive young son remembers the monster, his father.

Kenny Norwell—Has Corie's ex tracked down the family he once terrorized to reclaim what's his?

Mr. Wally Stinson—The building super has a key to everything in the building.

Jordy and Harve—A couple of guys who've had too much to drink.

Mark Taylor— Matt's younger brother is also a firefighter.

Amy Hall—Mark's fiancée plays matchmaker for her favorite future brother-in-law.

Cole Taylor—Matt's uncle is a KCPD detective whose investigation overlaps a series of fires that has been keeping Firehouse 13 busy.

Chad Meade—This second-generation mobster wants to reclaim his uncle's criminal empire.

Enrique Maldonado—Cole Taylor's confidential informant.

Chapter One

Smoke.

Kansas City firefighter Matt Taylor held the handles of the resistance weights in front of him, feeling the pull along his massive arms and broad chest. He turned his nose toward the doorway of the spare bedroom, where he worked out when he wasn't on duty at the fire station, and sniffed the air.

Definitely smoke.

Slowly, deliberately, he eased the cables back through the pulley system and let the weight drop down to the stack. He grabbed the towel off the floor beside him and wiped the sweat from his face and neck, then swiped it over the top of his dark, military-short hair before rising from the machine's bench. He was a lieutenant at Firehouse 13 now, and his years of training and natural low-key demeanor kept him from panicking as he stalked through his apartment and checked the usual suspect spots. Kitchen clean and clear. Furnace running efficiently despite it being two degrees and snowing outside. Even though he emptied it out faithfully, he opened the closet where the washer and dryer were stacked and checked to make sure there was no lint in the dryer vent.

No fire here.

But his nose never lied.

And then his ears tuned in to the distinctly high-pitched, repetitive beep of a smoke detector, muted by walls and distance.

The fire wasn't here.

Pulling the towel from around the neck of his gray KCFD T-shirt, he tossed it over the back of a kitchen chair and reached beneath the sink to pull out the small fire extinguisher he stored there. Sweats and running shoes were hardly standard gear to battle a fire, but he knew it was the man, not the equipment, that was his best weapon to locate and put out a blaze. Ready to do battle, he jogged to the door of his apartment and flung it open.

A woman screamed.

Corie McGuire, the single mom who lived across the hall, pressed a hand to the neckline of her navy cardigan sweater, her small chest heaving in and out as she huddled back against the door to her apartment. "Good grief, Mr. Taylor. Don't startle me like that."

"Where's the fire?" He was sharply aware of the panic rounding her mossy-green eyes that were tilted up at him, the fact she was keeping as much distance between them as the door at her back allowed, and the charred iron skillet she clutched with an oven mitt down at her side. The sticky residue in the bottom of the skillet was still smoking. Matt quickly kicked the welcome mat from in front of his door across the wood-planked floor. "Put it down."

She hesitated a few seconds before nodding. He'd spoken in a tone that people usually obeyed, and she did, kneeling to set the hot pan on the mat. "It will leave a mark on your— Oh. Okay." He sprayed foam on the skillet, pulled the mitt from her startled hand, and lifted the pan to spray the bottom and sides as well, ensuring whatever substance had burned inside it couldn't catch fire again. "Thank you. I was going to take it downstairs and set it in the snow beside the dumpster out back. Pitch it out in the morning before school. This works, too."

With the charcoal goop in the pan extinguished to his satisfaction, Matt stood the same time she did. And swallowed hard. Somehow, he had drifted closer to his neighbor, or she had moved closer to him, and her ponytail had brushed against the *So Others May Live* firefighting emblem tattooed beneath the sleeve on his upper arm. Objectively, he'd always known Corie McGuire was a pretty woman, probably about his same age, late twenties, early thirties. But he'd never been this close to her before.

He'd never felt this gut punch of awareness about her, either.

Beneath the scent of her shampoo, he detected something salty and sweet, like pancakes and syrup with a side of crispy bacon. Maybe not the sexiest scent to most men, but he found himself craving it. It was certainly a more enticing scent than the smoky haze seeping into the hallway from beneath her closed door.

"You have smoke in your apartment," he pointed out, switching off the man to stay in firefighter mode. "I can help."

"That's all right. I've opened some windows to air things out. Sorry if it bothered you." When she knelt to retrieve the skillet, Matt stuck out a warning hand, which she instantly straightened away from. "Leave it."

"Leave it?" She shook her head. "Mr. Stinson will hardly appreciate finding a burned mess in the middle of the floor."

Matt didn't care what the building super thought—he had a more immediate problem that needed to be dealt with. But he knew he wasn't handling tonight's encounter well. From the time he'd reached his full height of six feet five inches and started bulking up after high school, his adoptive mother and grandmother had gently warned him that people who didn't know him might find him intimidating. And though the women in his family knew he was more gentle giant than scary ogre, others, like Corie McGuire here, might misread his blunt demeanor and quiet ways and be afraid of him.

Not that he blamed her for giving him a wide berth. He was a big, scary dude. When he wasn't lifting weights, he was running, partly because the physical demands of his job meant he needed to stay in shape, and partly because he had little else to do, especially in the wintertime. Other than a Sunday dinner with his grandmother and some assortment of parents, brothers, uncles and their families once or twice a month, or an occasional trip to the bar after shift with his Lucky 13 firehouse buddies, he didn't really have a social calendar.

The top of Corie McGuire's blond head barely reached his shoulder, and the woman was built on the slender side of things. They'd exchanged little more than a nod in the elevator after she and her son had moved in across the hall. Even then, she kept her boy hugged close to her and shifted to wherever the opposite side of the elevator was from him. He'd helped carry her groceries up one time, and even then, she'd stopped at her door and had taken the bags without letting him into their apartment. Since he wasn't the most outgoing of people, he hadn't immediately noticed that she was right there with him, keeping neighbors at a polite distance and never having friends over. Now that he thought about it, the woman and her son kept to themselves pretty much. He should give her the space she seemed to want from him.

But there was a haze of smoke drifting into the hallway and a beeping alarm telling him something wasn't right. And one thing that Matt Taylor never shied away from was his job as a firefighter.

"This is what I do for a living. Would you mind if I came in and checked to make sure there are no secondary hot spots trying to ignite?"

If possible, Corie's eyes widened further. "There could be another fire?"

"You said you opened a window?"

To his surprise, she reached behind her to twist the doorknob, inviting him in. "My son is in here. Please."

The moment the door opened, the shrill beep of the

smoke detector pierced Matt's eardrums. Closing the door behind them, he followed her into the kitchen. Corie braced her hands over her ears as they walked beneath the archway where the smoke detector was blaring its warning. The smoke was thicker here, with a dirty-gray plume billowing out of the open oven. Matt wasted no time closing the oven door and moving past her to close the kitchen window. Then he reached up to pry the cover off the smoke detector and pulled out the battery. The sudden silence didn't immediately stop the ringing in his ears.

But Corie lowered her hands. "Thank you." She'd already turned the oven off, but he squatted in front of the appliance, peering through the rectangle of glass, looking for any stray sparks or glowing elements. "Is something still burning?"

"You want to keep the oven door shut and all the windows closed until you're certain the fire is out. A lot of fires reignite the moment you add fresh air to the mix." He watched for a full minute before he set the fire extinguisher he'd carried in with him on the counter. "I think we're good." She had leaned in beside him to study the oven, too. But he didn't realize how close she was, and he bumped into her when he stood. His instinct was to reach for her to keep her from falling, but she grabbed the edge of the countertop to steady herself and scuttled away to the kitchen archway to keep him from touching her. Matt let his hand drop back down to his side. "Sorry."

She growled and huffed a breath that stirred the wheat-colored bangs on her forehead, and he wondered if that was her version of a curse. "No. I'm the one who's sorry. You've never been anything but polite, and now you're trying to help us, and that was rude. I've already screamed at you once tonight."

"Self-preservation isn't rude. I startled you. You do what you need to do to feel safe."

"I…" Her lips parted to argue, but they snapped shut again. Her posture relaxed and she hugged her arms around her middle. And smiled. A real smile. The tension around her eyes relaxed, and her soft pink mouth curved into a grin. "Thank you for understanding."

He could point out that with his superior strength and longer legs, he could have reached out and grabbed her without any effort at all if that had been his intent. But why would anyone want to make that beautiful smile disappear? Especially when that smile was directed at him. It made him want to smile, too.

Um, what are you doing, Taylor? Sniffing your neighbor? Smiling at her? Stop it or you'll really scare her.

Turning away, Matt checked the oven one more time, assuring himself the fire was out and whatever had burned had been starved of the oxygen it needed. Instead of moving toward Corie and the archway, he crossed back to the kitchen window and opened it. Then he turned on the hood fan above the stove and waited to see if she would move out of his path.

"Is it safe to open windows now?" she asked, maybe just to break the awkward silence of him waiting for her to move.

Matt nodded. But when he heard the furnace kick on, he took a step toward her and the smile vanished. He quickly halted. She didn't need a firefighter anymore.

She needed a respectful neighbor who would finish his business here as quickly as possible and go back to his own apartment. "Where's your thermostat?" She hugged one edge of her sweater over the other, shivering at the cold night air filling the kitchen. "You might want to grab an extra sweater," he advised. "It'll take twenty, thirty minutes to get the smoke out of here."

She nodded. "Mother Nature hasn't exactly graced us with warm weather and sunshine. I loved having all this snow for Christmas. But it wouldn't hurt my feelings any if it warmed up and melted away and spring came early."

"Spring won't happen in January. Not in Missouri."

"You're right, of course." She grabbed her wool coat off the back of a chair and shrugged into it as she led him through the apartment. "This way."

Although the layout of her apartment was a mirror image of his own across the hall, and he could have found the thermostat on his own, his training as a KCFD firefighter had taught him that a woman alone at the scene of a fire of any size probably wouldn't appreciate a man barging through her personal space—unless the whole place was fully engulfed and him storming in meant the difference between life and death. So he politely followed her out of the kitchen, through the living room and down the hall.

Corie wore her ponytail high on the back of her head, and it bounced against her collar like a shaft of golden wheat swaying in the wind. There was a sway to her hips, too. He'd noticed how her jeans had curved with a womanly flare, but even with her heavy coat, her natural slenderness blossomed in all the right places.

Matt didn't realize his gaze was still plastered to her backside until she stopped at the hallway wall between the two bedrooms and a little boy with a longish mop of brown hair stepped out of the second bedroom. "What do you want?" He stepped in front of Corie and held up a beastly-looking blob built out of hard plastic blocks—a dragon, he'd guess, based on the plastic swirls of flame attached to the creature's snout and the triangular bits that were either short wings or Godzilla-like spines on its back. From behind the colorful creation, which he held up like a shield, the boy peeked up at Matt with green eyes that matched his mother's. "The fire will get you if you come too close."

"Evan!" Corie slipped her arm around her son's shoulders. "You remember Mr. Taylor from across the hall. He's our neighbor. Now be polite."

Matt had a little nephew who had mastered that put-upon eye roll. He also recognized the stance of a young man—even this slight little boy—protecting someone he cared about. He respected that reaction as much as he worried about being the cause of it. Evan McGuire tucked his homemade dragon beneath his arm. "Sorry, sir. Hi."

Matt was equally brief. "Hi." He adjusted the thermostat to a much lower temperature, waiting for the furnace to shut off.

If Corie McGuire barely reached his shoulder, her son, Evan, barely reached his waist. They must be built on the slim side of things in the McGuire family. Matt scarcely remembered his birth parents, but they had been tall and broad shouldered like him and his younger brother, Mark, who was also a firefighter with the Lucky 13 crew.

The boy's diminutive size didn't stop Evan from stepping forward, tipping his head back and sizing up their visitor. "You're big up close."

"I'm big far away, too." He parroted the phrase his petite grandmother had often teased him with.

Corie snickered at the joke. She snorted a laugh through her nose, then quickly slapped her hand over her mouth. She looked more embarrassed than he was by her noisy amusement. Whether it was for his sake or hers, she quickly hustled her son toward the hall tree by the front door. "Evan, get your coat on. It's going to get cold in here."

Matt recalled one elevator ride together where Evan had announced it was his eighth birthday before his mother had shushed him and ended any conversation before it got started. Like any self-respecting young man, he groaned at being told what to do, even as he tromped through the living room and pulled on an insulated jacket that had sleeves that were too short for his arms and that clung to his small frame as he zipped it up.

But his demeanor changed when he looked into the hallway and saw the ruined skillet on Matt's door mat. "I'm sorry, Mom. I didn't mean to make a mess. I tried to put the fire out."

"It's not your fault." Corie ruffled his hair and kissed the top of his head, ushering him back inside. "I should have ended my phone call with Professor Nelms and fixed you a snack myself so you didn't have to turn on that old oven."

"But I made the frozen pizza just the way you showed me."

"Then maybe there's something wrong with the oven. I'm just glad you weren't hurt."

He nodded. Then tipped his chin up to Matt. "I'm sorry we bothered you, Mr. Taylor." Evan glanced over at his mom. "Isn't that right?"

Matt glimpsed the sadness and regret that tightened her features before she forced a smile onto her lips that wasn't quite as pretty as the natural smile she'd shared in the kitchen. What made a child apologize for a simple, albeit potentially dangerous, mistake, and a mother regret that he felt he needed to apologize?

Matt had never been a parent, but he'd been raised by the two finest people he'd ever known. He remembered how his adoptive father, Gideon Taylor, had coaxed him out of his silence and fear as a traumatized orphan. He'd given Matt jobs to do, small responsibilities that he could succeed at and grow his self-confidence. Gideon Taylor had worked side by side with each of his sons, showing them what it took to be a good man, how to be part of a family, how to live in the world with a sense of purpose and not be afraid of doing the wrong thing. Again.

Emulating the lesson of his own dad, Matt unhooked the multidialed utility watch from his wrist and held it out to Evan. "Can you tell time?"

Evan scoffed a little snort through his nose, reminding Matt of the adorable sound his mother had made a few minutes earlier. "Of course I can. We learned that in first grade. I'm a second grader now."

"Good man. Take this." Evan's eyes widened as he looked at all the numbers for time, temperature and barometric pressure readings. His mouth dropped open before he took it from Matt's outstretched hand. "When thirty minutes have passed, I want you to turn this thermostat back up to seventy degrees and remind your mom to close the kitchen window. Can you do that?"

Evan danced with excitement. "Is that okay, Mom?"

"You'll have to give Mr. Taylor his watch back," she reminded him.

"Not for thirty minutes," Evan protested.

"It's not a gift."

"Please?"

Matt wasn't sure he'd be able to withstand the enthusiastic energy pouring off the boy. Corie smiled the good smile again. "All right. Homework done?"

"Yes, ma'am."

"Good. Then you can use that same half hour to play your game before bedtime."

Corie combed her fingers through his hair and cupped his cheek. When she started to kiss him again, he glanced up at Matt and pulled away, perhaps embarrassed by the PDA, perhaps trying to be more like the man he believed being trusted with Matt's watch made him. "Did I tell you I earned a ronin to fight with my dwarf? Now I can shoot arrows at the bad guys."

"That's great." She smiled again at her son's delight

over the video game Matt was familiar with. "Do you even know what a ronin is?"

But Evan was already dashing down the hallway past Matt into his room. "'Bye, Mr. Taylor. See you in thirty...twenty-nine minutes."

The furnace clicked off with a noisy jerk. Matt hadn't had this much conversation outside of work for a long time, and the urge to stay a little longer and keep talking with this tiny family felt odd. Didn't stop him, though. "Sounds like something my younger cousins have played. I've played it with my brothers, too, a few times. If I remember correctly, a shapeshifter and sorcerer are next to join the team."

"You play *Bomba's Quest*?"

Matt wondered if his cheeks were heating with a blush or if he was succumbing to some weird kind of hypothermia. "My uncle Brett wanted to know if it was appropriate for his kids to play. My brothers and I volunteered to test it."

"I wondered if it was appropriate for an eight-year-old, too. He likes figuring out the puzzles and solving the riddles. But the characters are all cartoons, and no one dies when they go to battle. Not like real violence where people get hurt." She stopped abruptly, as though she was surprised to hear herself say those words out loud. "I'm sorry. I'm rambling. I'll be sure to get your watch back to you. That was a nice gesture."

Matt was as curious about the shadow that crossed her features as he'd been about the things he'd said that had made her smile.

Get back to being a firefighter and get out of here.

"You make pizza in a skillet?" he asked, picking up on something her son had said.

"The cast iron heats up and works like a pizza stone. The handles should have made it easier for Evan to manage." When she headed back to the kitchen, Matt followed. "Usually, his go-to snack is popcorn in the microwave, but for some reason, my microwave isn't working tonight." She pushed a couple of buttons beside the handle, but nothing lit up. "I don't know if it's the microwave or the socket it's plugged into."

If her apartment was wired like his, there should be a circuit breaker on the microwave outlet. Possibly, it had tripped and neither Corie nor her son knew to push the button back in to reconnect the circuit. But an oven fire *and* a faulty microwave in one evening? That seemed to be an unusual amount of bad luck for anyone, especially a woman who seemed as competent and careful as Corie. Matt pushed the circuit breaker button, but nothing reengaged.

"I tried that already."

Good. So, she knew that safety measure. Either the microwave itself was broken or there was a problem with the wiring. Matt unplugged the appliance and moved it to the opposite counter where there was another plug.

"You don't have to do that. I'll call Mr. Stinson tomorrow to look at it. I'm sure you were busy doing something important."

The moment he plugged it in to the new socket, all the lights came on. "It's not the microwave. Looks like a wiring issue." He glanced over his shoulder to see

Corie frowning at the now-empty socket. "Is something wrong?"

"I'm not sure."

On a hunch, he asked her for a flashlight and then knelt in front of the oven again. After testing to make sure it wasn't hot to the touch, he rubbed his fingers along the heating elements at the top and bottom of the oven. A sticky, charred residue like what he'd seen in the skillet came off in his hands. He'd fought enough fires to know there was something unnatural about this one.

He tried not to jerk when he felt Corie's hand on his shoulder, balancing herself as she knelt beside him. "What's that?"

"I'm not sure." He could easily understand food overflowing its pan and spilling onto the heating element at the bottom of the oven. But something needed to be spraying oil or grease—and a lot of it—for it to coat the top heating element like this. And nothing about pizza sprayed when it baked. "Did you squirt anything on the fire to put it out?"

"Evan threw some flour on it."

"Flour burns."

"I know that. He knows that, too, now." She pulled her hand away and stood, opening the cupboard above the stove. "I keep a can of baking soda mixed with salt in here to put out small fires."

An old-school solution that worked as well as a chemical extinguisher. "It snuffs out the oxygen."

She nodded. "I showed Evan where I keep it and taught him how to use it. I was in my bedroom, on the phone with my professor about a project for my college class. I didn't realize there was a fire until the smoke detector went off. I ran out here, saw the flames, grabbed the can…" She opened the lid and handed him the can. There was only a dusting of powder at the bottom. "It's empty. That's why he went for the flour instead. The only time we've used the baking soda mixture was when I was teaching him how to put out a fire. I lit a match in a pan and had him put it out so he could practice. This should still be full. I don't know how…" A dimple formed between her eyebrows as she frowned. "I don't remember emptying it. I don't know why I would."

Maybe she hadn't.

Curious. And a little disturbing to think that all the safeguards she'd had in place to protect her son from a fire had failed.

Matt needed some time to ponder on that. Evan seemed to be a precocious little boy. And God knew Matt understood a child's fascination in playing with fire. But would an eight-year-old know how to sabotage an electrical outlet to make his story about using the oven plausible? Or was there something else going on here? For now, Matt simply wanted to complete his due diligence as a firefighter, and as a good neighbor. If there was anything he could do to help Corie feel safer in her own apartment—even if that meant him leaving—he would do it.

"My microwave works," he offered. "I'm at home on Tuesday nights. If he wants a snack, and you're busy with schoolwork, he could come over."

"Usually, he can safely occupy himself when I'm

studying. And he knows he can interrupt me if he needs something." She placed the empty can back in its cupboard. Then she pasted a tight smile on her face and headed to the front door. Did she suspect her son of setting the fire, too? "I'll show you out."

This time, he didn't follow. "You want me to move the microwave back, or leave it here?"

"Leave it. You've done enough."

He was beginning to think he hadn't done nearly enough. "Talk to the super. He needs to replace that stove and the microwave outlet before you use either one again."

"I will." She was waiting by the front door.

"Do you have a safe place to cook your meals in the meantime?"

"Afraid we're going to start another fire?"

He didn't joke about stuff like that. And judging by the frown dimple that had reappeared on her forehead, she wasn't trying to be funny, either.

What was going on here? Just a series of unfortunate coincidences that had taken their toll on a tired, hardworking single mom? Or did she share any of the same suspicion he did that something was deliberately off in this apartment tonight?

Finally, he forced his feet to move to the door. "I'll leave the fire extinguisher here until you get your baking soda solution restocked. I have another one in my truck." When he moved past her into the hallway, he picked up the torched pan and handed her the oven mitt. "I'll take this down to the dumpster for you."

Her fingers brushed against his as she tried to take the skillet from him. "You don't have to do that."

No way could she muscle the ruined pan away from him, but another unexpected touch like that, sending ribbons of unfamiliar heat skittering beneath the skin she'd made contact with, and she could probably ask him for anything she wanted. What kind of sorry, solitary soul was he to be so attuned to a woman he hadn't said ten words to before tonight? He pointed back toward the kitchen. "When I'm done, I'll come back to reset the smoke alarm. Evan's thirty minutes should be up by then."

"Okay." She hugged the door frame, her shoulders lifting with a sigh that made him think she was either too tired to argue with him, or just agreeing to whatever he said that would make him leave. "I'll lock the door behind you. Knock when you get back."

Matt carried the pan to the first floor and braved the cold air without a coat to set it on the dumpster behind their building. He spared a few minutes to pull his pocketknife from his sweats and scrape some of the residue from the bottom and handle of the pan. Although there were definitely bits of cheese and hamburger that had turned to ash, there was also more of that same sticky substance he'd found on the oven's heating element. He cut a swath of plastic from a trash bag inside the dumpster and wrapped the sample inside before stuffing both the knife and the sample into his pocket. This hadn't been a big enough fire, nor an official KCFD investigation, to warrant sending the substance to the state fire lab, but he could ask his firehouse captain and some of the other more experienced fire-fighters at the station house if they'd run across anything like it before. A bracing wind whipped through the alley, chilling him from his speculation.

On the way back inside, he paused in front of Wally Stinson's door and thought about asking the super if he'd worked on any of Corie's appliances or electrical outlets recently, or if she'd filed a complaint about any of them needing repairs. He'd like to ask if there had been any other small fires in the apartment, too—anything that might indicate a boy playing with matches or other flammable materials. But there was no sound coming from within the apartment, and there was no light shining from beneath the super's door, so the man had either gone to bed or was out for the evening. He'd make a point to stop by the next morning on his way to work.

Matt walked past the elevator and took the stairs, needing time to think. One strange thing in Corie's apartment he could dismiss as an accident. Two made him curious. But three missteps, all leading to a potentially dangerous fire and no way to fight it, told him something was wrong. Now whether Corie was really good at hiding irresponsible behavior, or something more sinister was happening behind the walls across the hallway, he couldn't say. In the meantime, Matt would do whatever he could tonight to ensure that Corie and Evan McGuire had nothing more to worry about and could get a good night's sleep.

By the time he'd reached the seventh floor, Corie was waiting outside her door, holding his watch and a small plate wrapped in plastic. "I went ahead and put the battery back in the smoke alarm myself. All I had to do was pull out a chair to reach it."

"You tested it?"

She nodded. "It beeped." In other words, *stop butting in, already*. She handed him the watch. "Evan says thank-you. I appreciate the way you eased his concern and made him feel useful. Although I didn't know what half the bells and whistles on this watch are for. And trust me, he asked about every one of them." After he'd strapped the watch back onto his wrist, she handed him the plate. "And here. It's not much. But thank you."

Matt didn't need a thank-you, and he certainly hadn't expected a gift. He lifted the plate to inspect the thick slice of cherry pie. He hadn't grown to 250 pounds of muscle by turning his nose up at a free dessert. But he felt awkward taking anything from this woman who wore a coat with a frayed collar, and whose son clearly needed some bigger clothes—and possibly some counseling on the dangers of playing with fire.

Misreading his hesitancy, Corie quickly apologized. "Don't worry. I didn't bake it in that rattrap of an oven. I work at Pearl's Diner evenings after school. Except on nights like this when I have class. Sometimes I bake, but mostly I wait tables."

He knew Pearl's. Classic diner food that filled your belly and made you feel at home. He'd eaten there with his family many times over the years. He knew the original owner, Pearl Jenkins, had retired and sold the restaurant to Melissa Kincaid, the wife of one of the detectives his older brothers, Alex and Pike, worked with at KCPD. But other than adding some lighter fare to the menu, he hadn't noticed any changes in the quality of the food. And the pie from Pearl's was legendary. "My boss lets me bring home any extra since we bake it fresh every day."

"You made this?"

Corie nodded.

He finally remembered his manners. "Thank you. Cherry's my favorite."

"I'm glad." She opened her door. "Well, thank you again. Good night, Mr. Taylor."

"Good night, Mrs. McGuire. Ms.? Miss?"

There was a drawn look to her features that spoke of fatigue. "I'm divorced from Evan's father. Corie will do just fine."

"Matt will do, too. For me. I'm Matt. Not married. Never have been. Never baked a pie."

She smiled in that way that made him feel like he hadn't just stuck his foot in his mouth and made an awkward conversation downright uncomfortable. "Good to know. Good night, Matt."

He waited in the hallway, hearing the dead bolt, a chain and the doorknob engage. He liked that she was cautious about her safety. Even though the City Market district was being reclaimed by Millennials and real estate investors, the transformation hadn't taken hold everywhere. The McGuires were still a lone woman and a little boy alone in the city.

And Matt was the scary dude across the hall who'd come out of his solitary refuge just long enough to save the day…and scare her back behind her tightly locked door.

Dragging his door mat back across the hall, he stepped inside his apartment and locked the door behind him. He'd return to his weights later. For now, he turned the TV on the late news, leaned back on the couch and stretched his feet out onto the table beside the takeout wrappers from tonight's dinner. He unwrapped the pie and inhaled its heady scent. Sweet and delectable, just like Corie.

Matt didn't even bother getting up to get a fork. He picked the wedge up in his hand and took a bite. His grandmother was one hell of a cook, and this pie reminded him of that perfect blend of talent and experience. The second bite made him forget the niggling thought at the back of his mind that told him something was very wrong in that small apartment across the hall.

There was also something very right about that little family.

Corie McGuire had pretty hair, a pretty butt and a pretty smile.

Matt inhaled the last of the sweet, flaky crust and tart filling.

And damn, the woman could cook.

He might just be in love.

Chapter Two

"Okay, now you're just showin' off."

Ignoring the teasing voice, Matt pushed up off the snow-dusted pavement after checking to make sure there was no fuel leak and pried open the hood of the burning car with his long-handled ax. He wedged it upward, bracing the ax between the frame and the hood to keep it open. He turned away from the billowing smoke that poured out over the fenders to frown at his younger brother, Mark, who'd brought a second ax from the engine parked several yards away in the parking lot.

"Huh?" Matt lifted the hose he'd dragged to the burning car off his shoulder and pointed it toward the flames before opening the valve and spraying the engine block. The steam of water meeting fire forced them both to take a step back. They wore their turnout gear like the rest of the Lucky 13 crew, who had responded to the call to a car fire behind an office building just north of the downtown area. But since this wasn't a structure fire they had to walk into where oxygen would be scarce, there'd been no call to wear face masks and a breathing apparatus. His cold cheeks stung with the spray of steamy moisture on and around his goggles, forcing Matt to redirect the water. "Are you complaining because I'm doing my job?"

"I'm complaining because you're doing everybody's job." Mark moved in beside him, waving his arm through the smoke and steam, clearing it away to get a visual on the origin of the fire to ensure that it was completely out. "Hell, I could have stayed at the firehouse where it's warm and finished my lunch instead of getting in the truck and riding here to watch you do all the work."

"I let you turn on the water and pressurize the hose, didn't I?" Matt covered the engine with one more spray of water before shutting off the valve and giving a high sign to Ray Jackson, another firefighter, who was waiting beside the hydrant to turn it off.

"Big whoop. I know this is small in the grand scheme of fires, but we are trained to work together as a unit. You're making me look bad in front of our adoring audience." Mark turned his blue eyes to the group of curious bystanders huddling together for warmth on the far side of the parking lot. "Unless you're trying to impress one of those ladies over there?"

Matt glanced across the way. Although he'd been aware of the small group of people, making sure they'd remained at a safe distance while he put out the fire, he hadn't really noticed that there were three women in the group. He didn't seem to notice any women since last night's visit to Corie McGuire's apartment. Honey-blond ponytails and big green eyes must be his thing. The two brunettes and a bright, unnaturally platinum blonde were attractive enough, he supposed, but not one of them had been compelling enough to divert his attention. "No."

"Of course not. Big bad Matt Taylor's just doing his job. Like always." Mark's groan echoed Matt's as Ray Jackson turned over shutting down the hydrant to another teammate and jogged across the parking lot to chat up the three ladies. "Can't say the same for Jackson."

"Maybe he knows one of them," Matt suggested, giving his teammate the benefit of the doubt.

"Would it matter if he did or didn't?" Mark swung his ax onto his shoulder and shook his head. "How am I ever going to find you a date to Amy's and my wedding if you got to compete with that?"

Matt shrugged as Ray took off his helmet and the three women eagerly shook hands with him. Matt had never possessed the gift of gab or the movie-star looks of their buddy Ray. He'd been a natural to represent Firehouse 13 on the KCFD fund-raiser calendar last year. Matt probably should be jealous. Instead, he was glad he'd never been called on to do any PR for the KCFD. Although he'd fought more dangerous fires than today's car fire side by side with Ray Jackson and was happy to let Ray or Mark do the friendly conversations with the witnesses and victims they interacted with, he was a little embarrassed to see Ray focusing squarely on the women in the group, barely acknowledging the two men standing with them.

"If we had a sister," Matt announced, "I'd never introduce them."

"Agreed." Mark clapped him on the shoulder, pulling his focus away from Ray and the onlookers and back to cleaning up after the fire. "Come on. I'll help you drain the hose and roll it back up. Water's freezing fast. Careful of that ice. I think we just turned this place into a skating rink."

They worked in silence for a few minutes while their firehouse captain, Kyle Redding, stood farther down the sidewalk talking with a uniformed police officer and the older couple walking their dog who had called in the burning car. Apparently, there was some issue in finding the owner of the vehicle. He'd like to think that Ray was following up on the investigation by chatting with the onlookers, but it didn't seem as though anyone who worked around here recognized the car or knew where the owner worked.

Matt pulled the hose out straight and began the laborious task of clearing the line before something Mark had said in jest—he hoped—sank in. "Don't set me up on any dates. Not even for the wedding."

Mark stopped abruptly and straightened, grinning from ear to ear. "Why? You seeing somebody I don't know about?"

Matt replayed the images of Corie walking away from him and the sweet smile that had softened her pretty mouth when he'd made her laugh. He wasn't sure exactly what he thought might happen with his neighbor. Probably nothing more than just that—being neighbors. But he wanted to savor last night's encounter with the small family across the hall awhile longer before he tried to work up interest in any matchmaking his brother and future sister-in-law might have in mind for him. "No. But I'm not interested in meeting anyone new."

Mark's blue eyes narrowed suspiciously. "So, you *have* met someone," he prodded, fishing for information.

Matt's answer was to pull off his goggles and toss them at Mark. "If you're so anxious to do some work, stop talking and get to it."

But Mark never gave up that easily. "Do I know her? Has anyone in the family met her? Did you find her on one of those dating sites?"

Matt gave the hose a strong tug, pulling it right out of Mark's hands. "I outrank you, Taylor," he teased, knowing with his brother, it was a useless threat. "I said get to work."

"Yes, sir, Lieutenant, sir." Although that cheesy grin never wavered, Mark had the good sense to let the matter drop so they could get the hose prepped for the truck.

Of Matt's three adoptive brothers, his younger brother, Mark, was the only one who was his brother by birth. Unlike their older brothers, Alex and Pike, who were cops, Mark had followed Matt into firefighting, making for a friendly family rivalry in interdepartmental softball games, blood drives and fund-raisers. Sometimes the cops won; sometimes the firefighters came out on top. But nothing could ever break the bond they shared. All four brothers had lived in the same foster home and had been adopted by Gideon and Meghan Taylor—the firefighters who had saved them in more ways than one, and who had inspired Matt to follow in their footsteps. The six of them had become the family that, as a child, Matt hadn't believed he'd ever find—or even deserved.

If Alex, the oldest, was their leader, and Pike, the second oldest, was the intellectual, then Matt was the quiet one. And that made Mark the obnoxious one. There was something about being the youngest—and something about being ridiculously in love and planning a summer wedding—that made Mark particularly ornery lately. Although he'd nearly lost his fiancée, Amy, to a serial killer who'd hidden his crimes in a series of arson fires, and had nearly lost his own life saving her, Mark was now as happy as Matt had ever seen him. Amy was good for Mark. She'd brought him out of his grief and guilt after the traumatic loss of their grandfather had hit Mark particularly hard—and she thought his goofy sense of humor was actually funny. No accounting for taste, he guessed.

Mark elbowed Matt's arm, drawing his focus back to the work at hand. "What's up with you today? I just caught you smiling. There *is* a woman."

"Nah. Not me." For now, Corie McGuire and her cherry pie were simply a good feeling Matt wanted to keep to himself. The musical trill of a woman laughing carried across the parking lot, and both Taylors paused to see Ray Jackson leaning in and saying something that delighted his captive audience. Knowing Ray, he'd have all their phone numbers before the conversation was over.

Mark snorted a laugh. "Maybe you and I ought to kick back and let Ray finish cleanup duty."

Matt shook his head, preferring to stay busy and

keep moving in the cold weather. He hefted his section of hose and carried it several feet closer to the fire engine. "What would you do if Ray flirted with your Amy like that?"

Mark followed with the next length of hose. "I love the guy. But I'd lay him out flat." Mark chuckled as he dropped the hose alongside the lines two other members of their team were winding onto the truck. "Unless Amy laid him out first."

Matt laughed with him, suspecting Mark's fiancée wouldn't put up with anyone or anything she didn't want to. Matt liked that directness about Amy Hall. Not only did it make it easy for him to have a conversation with his future sister-in-law, but her honesty left him with no doubt just how much she was in love with Mark. While Matt was a little envious that his three brothers had found their soul mates, and the two older ones had even started families, he was also happy that Alex, Pike and Mark had each found the right woman. One day, he hoped for the same.

He silently wondered if anything would come of this unexpected attraction to Corie, and if he could handle the ready-made family that came with her. Not for the first time since last night, Matt debated his suspicions about the oven fire in the McGuire apartment. He'd shown the residue he'd collected to Captain Redding this morning before they'd been called out, and the captain—who had almost twenty years of experience on Matt and agreed the substance was suspicious—promised to run it by some of his old cohorts in the department. Something was off about the whole story of baking a pizza gone wrong. Something more than the sooty remains of a fire had coated the heating elements in the oven. And Corie had seemed so certain that she'd had a fire-suppressant mixture stored in her cabinet for just such an emergency that he had a feeling there was something deliberate about that fire.

Somebody had wanted it to burn.

Matt had set more than one fire himself when he'd been barely more than a toddler. He'd been curious, yes, but he understood now that he'd been acting out against his birth parents' neglect, and later against being stuck in foster care and the guilt he felt at putting him and Mark there. Was there something going on in Evan McGuire's life that was making the eight-year-old experiment with fire? It would require Matt drawing on some painful memories, but maybe it was worth prodding Corie a little to see if she suspected her son might have picked up a dangerous hobby, and if he could get the boy some of the same type of counseling that had helped him as a child.

"Yo, Matt." Mark's summons pulled Matt from his thoughts. "Take a look at this." Mark was standing in front of the sedan's charred engine block. Now that the fire was out and the smoke and steam had dissipated, they could make a clearer assessment of what might have caused the fire, despite the ice frozen around the parts Matt had hosed with water. "You're the fix-it guy. Those wires don't belong there, do they?"

Matt frowned at the blackened metal wires crisscrossing above the radiator and battery. If they'd been part of the car's makeup, they should have been coated in rubberlike polymers or plastic to prevent sparks or accidental electrocution to the unwary handler. Even with the intense heat of the fire, some trace of the insulation should have remained. Reaching under his turnout coat, Matt pulled out his pocketknife and chipped away at the ice. "Looks like some kind of homemade repair job." He peered down between the frame and engine parts. "It doesn't look like they're holding anything together, though. Just a sec."

Without regard for the snow or ice, Matt dropped down to the ground and slid as much of his bulk as he could beneath the car. Between his flashlight and the pocketknife, Matt quickly found what the wires were attached to—the melted remains of a cell phone and a wad of charred, waxy cord that fed into a hole in the oil pan.

Talk about wanting something to burn.

This fire was no accident.

"Hey, if it isn't the wonder twins." At the sound of approaching footsteps and a man's familiar voice, Matt slid from beneath the car.

"Uncle Cole." Mark was already trading a handshake and friendly back-slapping hug with the dark-haired older man by the time Matt was on his feet.

"Mark. Matt." Other than the lack of silvering sideburns, Cole Taylor was a dead ringer for their father, Gideon.

"Uncle Cole." Matt reached out to shake hands with the family member, too. His gaze dropped to the KCPD badge and gun peeking out from beneath his leather jacket before sliding back up to slightly lined blue eyes. That meant he was on duty. It didn't explain why he was here at the scene of a small fire, though. "Good to see you."

He pointed to the man with the dark sideburns and stocking cap standing beside him. "This is Agent Amos Rand, my new partner. I'm showing him the ropes while my regular partner is on maternity leave. He's on temporary assignment from NCIS."

"A Navy man?" Matt extended his hand in greeting.

"Marines." Agent Rand could give Matt a run for the money in the stoicism department. But his grip was solid and friendly enough.

"Like Grandpa." Mark shook hands with Cole's new partner. "He served during the Korean conflict, and in the reserves for several years after that. He died earlier this year."

Matt reached over and squeezed his brother's shoulder. They all missed the family patriarch, who'd suffered a fatal heart attack while helping Mark rescue the victims of a car accident. But Mark seemed to take it personally that he hadn't been able to save their grandfather, as well.

Agent Rand buried his hands in the pockets of his coat and nodded. "I would have liked your grandpa."

"You would have loved Dad," Cole agreed, erasing the wistful grief that had momentarily darkened his expression. "He'd have been telling you stories for hours. A few of them might even have been true."

Amos chuckled. "Sounds like a good man."

"He was the best," Cole and Mark echoed together.

Matt nodded his agreement. "What brings you two

to our parking lot on this cold day? You're not working arson now, are you?"

Cole shook his head. "We're still major cases, organized crime division."

Amos pulled out his cell phone and nodded toward the sedan. "You all catch up." Matt watched the NCIS agent type in the license plate and send it off in a text before he circled around the car, sizing up the blackened engine block and peering into the windows. "This was an arson fire?"

"Looks like it," Matt confirmed.

Cole shoved his hands deep into the pockets of his coat, his breath gusting out in a cloud of warm air. "We're supposed to meet a CI on a case we're investigating."

"CI?" Mark asked.

"Confidential informant." Cole Taylor scanned the people around the parking lot before tilting his gaze to the windows above them on either side. "Don't suppose you've seen a skinny, hyperactive guy with dark hair? Possibly wearing coveralls. He works at a garage over on South McGee."

"We cleared the immediate area." Matt pointed to the gathering across the parking lot where one of the brunettes was typing on Ray Jackson's phone. "Except for that group over there, it's too cold to have a lot of onlookers. Is one of those men your guy?"

"In a suit? I don't think so." Cole glanced back as Captain Redding dismissed the couple with their dog. "The guy talking to your captain is too old to be our man. Our CI requested we meet on neutral ground where the chances of anyone recognizing him would be next to nil. He'd stand out like a sore thumb here in the business district. Unless he was dropping off some-body's car he was working on."

Amos returned from inspecting the car. "It's Mal-donado's car," he confirmed. "Plates and VIN number are in his name."

"Ah, hell." Cole looked up at Matt, his expression grim. "Please tell me you didn't find a body in it?"

"Hadn't looked beyond the front and back seats."

"Can you open the trunk?" When Matt hesitated, Cole pulled back the front of his coat to expose his badge where anyone passing by the scene could see it. "We have probable cause that our man could be in dan-ger. I'll take full responsibility."

"Not a problem." His firefighter's training included a vow to save people before property. Since Matt's ax was currently wedged between the hood and frame, Mark picked up his ax and followed them to the back end of the car. He wedged the blade into the locking mechanism and forced it open. Suspecting it was use-less to warn the two officers to stay back, Matt raised the trunk. Although some of the smoke from the engine has made its way through the car's interior and drifted out to dissipate in the wintry air, it was easy to see that there was nothing inside but the spare tire and a tool-box. "The car looks abandoned." He reached inside to open the toolbox. "He's got the means here to rig that fire. But then, it wouldn't take any special tools to set that up. Just a cell phone and the know-how."

Cole and Agent Rand went into investigator mode,

snapping pictures of the vehicle with their phones and sending the information on to a third party—a fellow investigator or someone in the crime lab, he guessed.

"This fire was no accident." Matt led his uncle to the front of the car to point out the ignition device beneath the hood. Amos took a picture of the cell phone itself and then dropped it into an evidence bag from another pocket of his coat. "I figured it was some kind of insurance scam. Abandoned car. Remote ignition. Whoever set it only had to call the number on the cell. Like striking a match in the oil pan. A spark, oxygen and fuel to burn. Ignition 101."

Agent Rand stood on the other side of Cole and tucked his phone away. "You think Meade's people are sending him a message—keep your mouth shut or you'll be in the car next time it burns?"

"Meade?" Mark frowned at the name from Kansas City's storied criminal history. "I recognize that name. You mean Jericho Meade and his mob connections? I thought he was dead."

"Alleged mob connections. And he is." Cole shook his head. "Tori and I took care of them."

Matt had heard the story of the undercover op several years earlier where Uncle Cole had met his wife, then–FBI agent Victoria Westin. They'd both infiltrated the crime family and had been forced to become allies to protect each other's cover and complete their respective missions. Pretending to be a couple had become the real thing. They'd both left undercover work once they'd gotten married and had their twin girls. And though Cole had remained a detective with KCPD, Tori had retired from the FBI to manage a small art gallery and focus on their girls.

Cole reached up with a gloved hand to smack Matt's shoulder, including both him and Mark in the point he was making. "But, just like the next generation of Taylor clan brothers are fighting to keep Kansas City safe, we believe the next generation of Meade's crime family is fighting to regain their influence. Jericho's nephew Chad Meade was released from prison after seventeen years a few months back. He's trying to take up where his uncle left off. Our CI was going to confirm that Meade has been stealing cars and sending them to a chop shop. Auto theft may be old-school, but we suspect he's using those profits to finance his efforts to bring illegal arms into the city. And using some legit businesses to launder money for suspected terrorists." He nodded toward Agent Rand. "That's the connection that brought NCIS into our investigation."

Mark frowned at what Matt suspected was a glossed-over version of Meade's criminal enterprise. "All that's going on in KC? In *this* neighborhood? There's a lot of money here. I thought this was where the Millennials and old-school yuppies worked and tore down old buildings to put up condos."

"They do." Cole pointed to the office building where the curious crowd had come from. "This isn't gang turf, but there are a couple of import/export and agricultural distribution companies headquartered in that building that we're monitoring. With KCI Airport and the Missouri River carrying so much traffic, Kansas City is considered a port city. That's why we've got all the embassies and customs offices here."

Agent Rand nodded. "Making it a hub for supply lines and money changing hands if the right man establishes a foothold here."

Mark snorted at the enormity of what Chad Meade was trying to accomplish after his stint in prison. "You mean the wrong man." He looked around the parking lot, tall buildings and crowd of suits and dresses that was dissipating now that the excitement of the fire was over and Ray Jackson had rejoined the team stowing gear on the trucks. "Although this would be a great neighborhood to find some nice cars to steal."

"Exactly. Not where our mechanic would be hanging out. We thought it'd be a good location to meet our CI." Cole studied the burned-out car again. "Apparently, someone else didn't agree."

Organized crime in their neighborhood? Were there really terrorist connections in the Firehouse 13 district? Matt thought of Corie and Evan McGuire, slight of build, super cautious and all alone in the world. Their building was about nine blocks from here—a bit of a long walk, but certainly doable. And Pearl's Diner, where Corie worked, was just around the corner, less than two blocks away. Several of the people working in these office buildings had probably eaten their lunch there. Maybe he should be worried about how safe any of them were.

"And you think this fire could have been set as a deterrent to your informant speaking out against Meade?" Matt asked.

Cole shrugged. "No proof one way or the other yet. Your first instinct could be right, and this is an insurance scam. If Maldonado had a change of heart, he could be looking for some quick cash from an insurance payout, or he could have torched the car to throw Meade's men—and us—off his trail. He'd have the know-how to rig a car like that."

Amos Rand shifted on his feet, looking anxious to leave. "I'd sure like to get eyes on him. Find out if he's had a change of heart, or if Meade's people got to him. Make sure he's still in one piece somewhere."

Two mysterious fires in two days. Not that Corie McGuire would have any connection to a police informant and organized crime. Matt suspected her son, left to his own devices for entertainment last night, had been playing with setting a fire. This burned-out car couldn't have anything to do with that.

It had to be a coincidence.

Not that he liked coincidences. But Matt was paid to put out fires and save lives, not solve cases for his uncle or anyone else in the police department.

"You okay, big guy?" Cole asked, pulling Matt from his thoughts. "You seem distracted."

Mark grinned like the annoying little brother he was. "That's what I said. I think there's a woman involved."

Matt slid him a warning glance. "Shut up."

That big grin must be a family trait. Cole matched Mark's amused expression. "Definitely a woman judging by that reaction."

Matt wasn't ready to admit to any emotion he wasn't

sure he understood yet. "Can't a man get any privacy in this family?"

But Mark wouldn't let it go. "Hey, you're the only Taylor bachelor left until our cousins graduate from high school and college. After being the baby brother for so many years, it's only fair that I get to pick on you for a change."

"Some things never change," Cole agreed. "Mitch, Brett, Mac, Gideon and Josh used to give me grief about finding a woman and settling down. Even Jess found a husband before I met your aunt Tori." He squeezed Matt's arm, offering some hard-won advice. "It'll happen when it happens. And it'll be worth the wait. But if there is somebody special, you know we'd all like to meet her. Whenever you're ready."

"Taylors!" Captain Redding shouted. He answered the dispatch summons on his radio before heading over to the first fire truck. "We got another call!"

Mark swore. "This whole neighborhood is turning into a dead man district."

"What does that mean?" Agent Rand frowned.

Matt explained the terminology. "A dead man zone is the spot where we suspect a fire will shift and spread to, given wind conditions, structural composition and so on. It's the place you *don't* want to be because the fire is coming your way."

Amos nodded with grim understanding. "You're saying this whole neighborhood is a danger zone."

"Yes."

Cole stepped back, reaching out to shake Matt's and Mark's hands again before sending them on their way.

"Go do your job. We'll work the crime scene here and copy you on anything we find out. You boys be safe."

Mark traded a quick hug before he and Matt jogged on past him. "Say hi to Aunt Tori and the girls."

"Will do. Hey, are we getting an invitation to your wedding?"

Mark turned, backing toward the engines. "They should go out next month. Amy's designing and making them herself. She's not just an artist, she's a perfectionist."

"She and Tori should have a lot to talk about at the next family get-together."

"Taylors!" Redding shouted from the captain's seat in the truck.

Matt tugged on Mark's coat. "Gotta go."

He doffed a salute to Cole and Amos before climbing up to his seat behind the steering wheel of the fire engine and starting it up. "What's up?" Matt asked.

The captain was still on his radio across the cab of the truck. "Class B fire at the recycling plant on North Front Street." Class B meant flammable liquids—several steps up in danger from an engine fire one man could put out. The recycling plant would definitely be a dead man zone if they didn't get there quickly enough.

All thoughts of Corie, Evan and mysterious fires he couldn't yet explain had to be put on hold.

"Let's go." Matt shifted the engine into gear and turned on the lights and siren. "Lucky 13 rolling."

Chapter Three

"Mom, if we had a watch like Mr. Taylor's, you could set the timer on it, and you wouldn't have to keep checking your watch every minute to see if we get home by my bedtime." Evan hopped from one foot to the next, following Corie down the aisle and off the bus. "Or we could use it to check the temperature to see if I need to wear my mittens and hat."

The bus door opened, and the damp, wintry night air slapped her in the face. Corie pulled her scarf snug around her neck and flipped up the collar of her coat before turning to her son and tugging his knit stocking cap down around his ears. "I don't need a fancy watch to know you have to wear your mittens and hat."

She looked over his head to Mr. Lee, the bus driver, who grinned from ear to ear at her son's persistent, supremely logical argument on the merits of buying a fancy watch for his next birthday, which was nearly a year away. "Good luck with that one," he said before bidding her good-night. "He'll keep you on your toes."

"That he will." She felt lucky and a little sad that the affable older gentleman who drove them home from

the diner nearly every night was one of the most familiar faces she knew in Kansas City. Other than her
coworkers at the diner and Evan's school, where she
worked as a para-educator until she finished her teaching degree, she hadn't made any effort to form friend-
ships since moving across the state. Not since her last
new *friend* in St. Louis had turned out to have a connection to her ex-husband, and she discovered Denise
had been feeding Kenny Norwell information about
her work and school schedule, and she ended up getting an unwanted and unfriendly surprise visit from
Kenny at the sports bar where she'd waited tables one
night. It was one of the few times she'd been glad Evan
was spending the night at her mother and stepfather's.
That visit from Kenny and the subsequent lecture from
her mother about blowing her chance at a reunion with
the man whose money and connections she liked more
than his treatment of her only daughter had been reason enough to transfer her college credits and move to
Kansas City. "Good night, Carl."

Corie stepped off the bus, wishing she had on jeans
or slacks instead of her waitress uniform. At least her
sturdy support shoes allowed her to move quickly so
that she didn't have to spend any longer than necessary
out in the cold air. She reached for Evan's hand and,
as soon as the bus pulled away from their stop, they
hurried across the street and down the two blocks that
would take them to their building.

Evan danced along beside her, full of energy after
spending four hours obediently sitting at a corner table
in the diner, completing his homework, eating dinner

and playing a game on her phone. "Honestly, if it's any help, I don't mind staying up past nine o'clock."

"I appreciate the offer," she teased. "But I know how impossible it is to get you up for school in the morning if you're up too late the night before."

"Or I could get a new watch," he countered. "My birthday's coming up in November."

"How about we just hustle for now, little man." She tightened her grip around Evan's hand and matched his eager pace.

If she could afford a Swiss Army Knife–like watch like Matt Taylor's, she'd be spending the money on a new, warmer coat that fit her son better, making a down payment on a cheap car so they wouldn't have to wait at a bus stop or walk these last two blocks in the open air, or, what the heck, maybe pay a bill or something. Making it completely on her own in the world was proving to be more rewarding than she'd imagined, even though it was sometimes a challenge to make ends meet. Even though a single phone call back to St. Louis would instantly fill her bank account, the help came with too many strings attached. Strings she had no intention of ever reconnecting.

Her life was here now, in Kansas City with her son. It might be a small life. But it was a good one. They were safe. Evan was growing stronger and more confident every day. And she believed—she hoped, at least—that one day they could have a normal life and be happy.

Corie's sigh formed a white cloud of air, and Evan slowed down to play at making clouds with his warm breath. Even though she played along to see how big

they could make a cloud before it chilled and dissipated, she kept Evan moving beside her, worrying as
much about his exposure to the cold air as their safety.

Fortunately, there was a bus stop on the same block
as Pearl's Diner, and bus passes were cheap. But she
worried about the January night air on Evan's young
lungs and every alley or parking garage they had to
walk past before they got safely inside the locked lobby
of their building. She wasn't above scoping out the
driver of every vehicle that passed, either, checking
to make sure her ex-husband hadn't made tracking her
down to their new apartment in a new city his top priority since his release from prison in Jefferson City eleven
months earlier. He'd contacted her through her attorney
in St. Louis demanding visitation rights with Evan, but
a firm no and a reminder of all the custody papers and
restraining orders she had in place had been her only
reply. Being told no wouldn't have made Kenny happy,
but Evan's panicked reaction to the possibility of seeing
his father—even under the parameters of a supervised
visit—had made her decision quick and easy. Corie's
job was to protect her son from the man he only remembered as a monster. She hadn't even given her estranged
mother her new name or address, and she hadn't listed
her new phone number. Their life in St. Louis felt like
a lifetime ago, but the wariness of her surroundings
and the potential threat of that past catching up to them
was as fresh as the diner's cheesy burritos for tomorrow morning's breakfast she carried in her backpack.

Since the lobby of the building was locked 24-7, she
had her key card ready to swipe as soon as they climbed

the granite steps and reached the outer glass doors. It was noticeably warmer the moment the door closed behind them, blocking the wind. Corie's stress level went down, as well, as soon as she heard the lock clicking into place. Once she and Evan got through the interior door, she inhaled a deep, calming breath, unbuttoned the top of her coat and loosened her scarf.

She considered stopping at Mr. Stinson's apartment while they were here on the first floor, but Evan had already run ahead to press the call button on the elevator. Nodding in silent agreement that her son had a better plan than knocking on the super's door, Corie followed Evan to the elevator, catching his mittens and cap as he shed them and stuffing them into the pockets of his backpack. Not that his energy level was showing any signs of ebbing, but she'd stayed late at the diner to fix their to-go breakfast and had missed their regular bus. Getting Evan to calm down and fall asleep by his nine o'clock bedtime was a challenge, even without the late start to his nightly routine. Mothering first. She'd run back down to see about the state of the oven and electrical outlet once she got her son in his pajamas.

Corie grabbed Evan by the shoulder when the elevator doors opened, checking the interior before following him inside the empty car. When the doors opened onto the seventh floor, Evan skipped down the hallway, leaving Corie to hurry after him. "Can I open it, Mom?"

Evan's fascination with gadgets, even one so simple as a key in a lock, gave her a moment to glance over her shoulder to the door across the hall. She idly wondered if Matt Taylor was home this evening. He'd said he usually had Tuesdays off, but what about Wednesdays? And just what did he do behind that door? Watch sports on TV? Work out? Maybe he was a gourmet cook or a fix-it guy with some carpentry or painting project going on. Was he into fast cars or monster trucks? Maybe he read books.

Evan pushed the door open and tossed her the keys, running inside to shed his coat and dump his backpack on the couch. Corie shook her head and followed him inside.

It didn't matter what Matt Taylor did behind closed doors. She had plenty to deal with right here inside *this* apartment. "Hey, little man." She turned the dead bolt behind her and nodded to the coatrack beside the door. "Hang up your coat and take your backpack to your room. You know we don't leave a mess in the living room."

"Yes, ma'am."

Corie was dragging with the length of her day after working two jobs, knowing she still had to get on her laptop to do more research for the paper she was writing for next week's class. But Evan happily bopped from one spot to the next, hanging up his coat and dashing down the hall to his bedroom before she even got her coat unbuttoned. "Get your pajamas on. Do you need a snack before you brush your teeth?"

"Can I have chocolate milk?" he shouted from his bedroom. From the sound of things, he'd opened a drawer in his toy chest and was riffling through his collection of tiny plastic building bricks to add to the ever-expanding fantasy fortress he was building on the table that had once been his desk. While she worried about the significance of her son building defensive fortresses and attack dragons, the school counselor insisted they were healthy outlets for the fears he'd carried with him since he'd been a toddler. "Cookies, too?"

"One or the other," she hollered back. "Pj's before playtime, okay?"

She smiled at his answering multipitched groan, picked up her own backpack and carried it to the kitchen. She flipped on the light switch and stopped in her tracks. "What the…?"

Her oven was missing. Not blackened up the front edge. Not under repairs. Gone.

"What…? Where…?"

Before she picked up the phone to call Mr. Stinson and ask how she was supposed to cook breakfast in the morning, Corie forced herself to inhale a steadying breath. What she noticed then wasn't much better.

She sniffed the air again. Something smelled off. Different. Extra.

Then she spotted the sticky note clinging to her microwave oven. She set her bag on the counter beside it and tore it off. She read it quickly, read it twice before breathing a little easier.

Mrs. McGuire—
    Got the plug fixed. Don't know how, but the wires had disconnected. The microwave works.
    Your oven will take me a little longer.
    We need to talk.
    Wally S.

"You're darned right we need to talk."

She crumpled the note in her fist and punched a couple of buttons on the microwave, just to reassure herself that she could heat up breakfast. Then she pushed up the sleeves of her cardigan sweater and got busy putting away the takeout box and cleaning up the mess of rearranged items and a grease smudge Mr. Stinson had left behind. She wiped down the countertops and found a space underneath the sink where she could move the pots and pans he'd taken from the bottom drawer of the oven and strewn across the counter. Then she pulled the sweeper from the pantry closet and swept out the dust bunnies that had collected under and behind the stove. She knew she should be feeling grateful for Mr. Stinson's help instead of this nagging sense of violation. But how could she explain to the kindly older gentleman the sense of intrusion she felt knowing that someone had been in her apartment while she'd been away?

He didn't know her history. No one in Kansas City did. Not all of it. He thought he was being helpful, doing his job. Wally Stinson *was* being helpful. She was the one whose sense of *friendly* and *helpful* and *normal* had been skewed by her ex-husband's violence and control, and her mother's opinion that everything Kenny had done to her was just part of being married. Even when he'd been arrested for multiple counts of arson and witness intimidation and had taken a plea deal that guaranteed his guilt in exchange for less prison time, Corie's mother had begged her not to divorce him. Kenny had money and connections and a veneer of status her mother accused her of throwing away.

Corie had dropped the charges of domestic battery and attempted kidnapping, just to make sure Kenny went away and she got full custody of Evan.

But any sense of security was fragile and hard-won. Yes, she'd broken all ties with Kenny and her mother. She'd moved away, changed her and Evan's names and lived as invisible a life as possible. But that didn't mean she still didn't jump at shadows, worry when Evan was out of her sight, and fear the idea of someone watching her, touching her things without her knowing, trespassing on her life.

She'd called Mr. Stinson this morning, and he'd promised to stop by. The man had keys to get into every apartment in the building. She'd *known* he would be here today. A normal person wouldn't be upset by that. Oh, how she desperately wished for the day she could feel normal again. Her therapist in St. Louis had advised her to visualize what she wanted her life to look like in the future, and eventually she'd be able to let go of the past and she'd get there. During her counseling sessions, she'd also learned to think before reacting. Her feelings of fear and distrust were to be expected, given all she'd been through. But that didn't mean she had to act on them.

Take a deep breath.

Think. Observe. Assess.

Then react to what was really here.

Corie did just that, taking the time to put away the sweeper and calm her fears. The building had been locked. Their apartment was locked. She and Evan were safe.

Mr. Stinson's presence accounted for the whisper

of an unfamiliar scent that lingered in the air. She squeezed her eyes shut and tried to pinpoint the fading smell of something woodsy combined with citrus. She opened her eyes and ran the water in the sink to rinse her dish rag. When she squirted the lemony hand soap to clean her hands, she thought she'd solved the mystery. Mr. Stinson had probably washed his hands here when he was done working. Moving the oven would have required a dolly and maybe some extra help from the part-time super who lived in the apartment below hers and helped with bigger projects like replacing a damaged oven.

But to completely dismiss her suspicions, Corie needed to do a little more investigating. Did the super wear cologne? Did his assistant? She wanted to verify that the extra scent in her kitchen belonged to one of them and her paranoia was simply an overreaction. It was yet another reason to get Evan into his pajamas and hurry downstairs to speak to the building super before he turned in for the night.

As she picked up a towel to dry her hands, her gaze landed on the dessert plate sitting in the drainer beside the sink. Matt Taylor had returned it early that morning, washed and dried, before heading to his shift at Firehouse 13. Since she and Evan had been in their usual mad dash to get ready for school and up to the bus stop, she'd thanked him again, thanked him for comparing her pie to his grandmother's and then, realizing the silliness of their rushed morning conversation, had told him goodbye and set the plate in the drainer before running back to her room to throw on some mascara, blush and lip gloss, grab their coats and backpacks, and get them up to the bus stop.

But that silly conversation at her door meant that Matt had been at her apartment twice now in the past twenty-four hours. Maybe that's what felt off about the apartment tonight. Other than the movers and Mr. Stinson, who was old enough to be her father, she hadn't had any man in here. Did Matt have a scent that lingered in the air? Somehow, she had the impression that he wasn't a cologne kind of guy. But that didn't mean he didn't put off natural pheromones that spoke to something purely feminine inside her. Was she just projecting her thoughts, imagining something had changed in her apartment because an attractive man had been here?

Corie put the plate away and leaned against the edge of the sink, staring at her reflection in the window there. She looked a little older and a lot more tired since the last time she'd thought of any man as attractive. She hadn't thought about a man that way in years. Not since Kenny and their ugly divorce. Not since remaking her life to keep her and Evan safe.

She was human enough to objectively appreciate a good-looking man, even to be a little bit in awe of the utter masculinity of size and strength embodied by her neighbor, especially in that sharply pressed, shoulder-hugging black firefighter's uniform he'd been wearing this morning. The day she and Evan had moved in, and they'd first met Matt Taylor, she had to admit, she'd been afraid of him. Her ex-husband, Kenny Norwell, was of average height and build, and he'd been scary enough when he'd used his words and his fists and his

threats against her. Sharing the close quarters of an
elevator ride with Matt had made her feel practically
helpless. She appreciated him respecting her need to
keep her distance. She'd never heard him swear or raise
his voice in anger. Over the months they'd shared the
same apartment building, she'd deduced that he wasn't
a seething powder keg about to blow, that he was truly
a quiet, gentle-natured person, despite his size.

Still, she'd been feeling like something was off in her
apartment for a couple of days now, even before Matt's
suspicions about the oven fire had reinforced her own
and made her anxious to get him out of her space, no
matter how kind and helpful he was being. The cherry
pie had been as much an apology for her sudden haste in
getting rid of him last night as it had been a thank-you
for allaying her fears about the fire. And for impress-
ing Evan with the watch and timekeeping responsibility.
Being estranged from her mother and stepfather meant
there was no strong adult male influence in Evan's life,
other than a couple of wonderful teachers. And she certainly wasn't going to get involved with another man
just to give her son a father figure. She'd learned the
hard way that marrying a man didn't make him a good
father—or husband.

Corie reached across the sink to pull the curtains shut
and cancel out both her perpetually wary expression
and the cold night beyond. Maybe she could ease up a
little on her isolationist rules that had become second
nature to her and strike up a friendship with Matt. Just
so Evan could have him as a friend, too.

Only, she had a feeling that Matt might be interested

in more than friendship. And she couldn't give him that. At least, she thought she'd felt those vibes of attraction, felt the heat of a wandering gaze plastered to her backside. And her mouth.

She couldn't even remember the last time she'd been kissed. The last time she'd wanted a man to kiss her.

Then again, she was so out of practice with relationships that she could be reading Matt Taylor all wrong. Matt was a quiet man who kept mostly to himself. As far as she could tell, there was no woman in his life. He was all about his work. And clearly, he worked out. Muscles like his didn't just happen. She'd seen him coming home in his black KCFD uniform or wearing a KCFD T-shirt like the one that had stretched across his broad chest last night often enough to know he was a firefighter, even before he'd announced it in the hallway last night. He was polite, a little awkward when it came to conversation, completely unaware of, or maybe embarrassed by, his dry sense of humor. But was he shy? Or was he reclusive for other reasons like she was?

Corie hung up the towel and headed out of the kitchen toward the bedrooms to make sure Evan was getting ready for bed. Certainly, she counted a few men among her friends—coworkers, classmates at Williams University. But they were more acquaintances than anyone she'd feel comfortable hanging out with in her own home. And nothing with them had ever fluttered with interest, much less real desire. Abuse, blackmail and living in fear of her and Evan's lives had made trusting a man impossible—and being attracted to one too big a risk to take.

She barely recognized the womanly impulses inside her anymore, but last night, something had definitely fluttered. Matt had sensed she was in danger and had come to her rescue. He'd taken several practical steps to keep her and Evan safe and to prevent any further damage to her kitchen and apartment. And he'd done it all without grabbing her, threatening her or talking down to her like she was an idiot who wouldn't understand.

Although Corie doubted she'd ever feel completely safe again after surviving her marriage to Kenny, for a few minutes last night, she hadn't been afraid. She'd been worried that Evan could have seriously injured himself, and that she'd have to dig into her meager savings to come up with the money to replace the oven if the super and building owner blamed her for negligence and didn't feel like replacing it. She'd even been unsettled by her suspicions that the fire hadn't been an accident.

But she'd felt safe with Matt Taylor in her apartment, taking up a lot of space, taking care of them, smelling like a man and saying unexpectedly silly things that made her want to laugh. She'd felt safe right up until the familiar survival instincts that had kept her alive for more than eight years had taken hold, and even the temptation of touching hard muscle and the warm skin of that tattoo peeking from beneath the sleeve of Matt's T-shirt had faded beneath her need to protect Evan and herself at all costs.

She couldn't indulge these rusty sensations of sexual awareness that had awakened inside her. But those few minutes of feeling safe, of feeling like a woman, of picking up the subtle signs of a man being interested in her, had been worth at least a slice of cherry pie.

Reaching Evan's room, she knocked softly on the doorjamb and stepped inside. He was already in his pajamas and building on his fortress. Surveying the whirlwind that was her son determined to have fun without disobeying her, Corie shook her head. She picked up his backpack from where it had hit the floor and set it in the desk chair before gathering up his discarded clothes and dropping them into the clothes basket inside his closet. She folded the sweater he'd been wearing and hugged it to her chest, hating to interrupt the bad guys attacking the ramparts of the castle and the dragon lord, or whatever that winged creature was he'd created, raising the towers ever higher in the battle of Evan's desk. But she needed to settle her fears. She opened the drawer of his dresser and set the sweater inside. "Hey, sweetie. You haven't opened a new soap or sprayed some of my perfume in the apartment, have you?"

The dragon swooped down and knocked over several tiny block warriors as he answered. "Ew, no. I don't like any of that girly stuff."

"Did you spill anything in the kitchen this morning?"

Evan pushed to his feet, his saving-the-world game momentarily forgotten as his sweet face aged with a frown. "Mom, is something wrong? I know the rules. I wouldn't break them. I know we have to stay safe now that Dad's out of prison. I haven't even told any of my friends my real name."

Oh my. Corie's heart hurt at the maturity she heard in Evan's voice.

"Evan McGuire *is* your real name now. Remember? The judge in St. Louis said so." Her mistakes and fears had forced her little boy to grow up way too soon. She crossed the room to wrap him up in a hug, cradling his head against her breasts and stroking her fingers through his shaggy brown hair. "It's okay, sweetie. I'm okay. I'm sorry if I worried you. Mr. Stinson removed the oven from the kitchen, and it's kind of throwing me off."

He let her hug him for about as long as an eight-year-old who thought he needed to be the man of the house could stand. He pushed away, tilting his wise green eyes up to hers. "I know you don't like changes in your routine. But I didn't do anything." He crossed his finger over his heart. "I swear." He glanced over at his sprawling stronghold. "I dragon swear."

Truly, the strongest vow that Evan McGuire could give. To his way of thinking, nothing could get past the dragon protecting them. If only reality could be as assuring as what this medieval fantasy world had become for her son.

"I'm not blaming you. I just wanted to check." She spared a couple of minutes to admire his dragon beast and the newest turret on his castle before catching a glimpse of the time. "You finish getting ready for bed. Remember to set the timer when you brush your teeth. I'm going to run downstairs and talk to Mr. Stinson for a minute. When I get back, we can read another chapter of that fantasy book together, okay?"

"Okay!"

With her son excited like the little boy he should be,

darting off to the bathroom to do her bidding, Corie grabbed her keys from her bag. She locked Evan in and took the elevator downstairs. When her knock on the superintendent's door produced no response, she followed the sound of men's voices out the back door of the building.

A cold wind whipped through the alley, wrapping Corie's polyester dress around her thighs and cutting through to her skin. Shivering as she stepped around the corner of the row of dumpsters, she found Matt Taylor crouched in front of what had once been her oven, with the building super leaning over his shoulder, shining a flashlight inside the appliance. Corie overlapped the front of her cardigan, clutching it together at her neck. "Mr. Stinson?" Matt instantly pushed to his feet and the superintendent stepped back, momentarily blinding her with his light before he pointed it toward the snow blowing across the asphalt. Corie tried to see what they'd been in such rapt conversation about, but she mostly saw a charred black hole. "Can't it be repaired?"

If she wasn't mistaken, Matt shifted his position to block the bulk of the wind. Not that she would warm up anytime soon, but at least she wouldn't get any colder. It was a thoughtful gesture. "Did you get a hot dinner?" he asked, forgoing any sort of greeting and *not* answering her question.

Corie nodded. She was more interested in what the two men had been discussing than the temperature of the nighttime air or the condition of her stomach. "Evan and I ate at the diner. Does this mean the oven can't be fixed?" She dropped her gaze from Matt's steady dark gaze to Mr. Stinson's disconcerting frown. "Do I have to pay for a new one?"

While she was calculating how many extra shifts she'd have to pick up to pay for a new appliance, Mr. Stinson cleared his throat. That didn't bode well. He rubbed his hand over the top of his balding head, then stepped back to gesture to the space between the dumpster and recycling bin. "Does your son like to play with matches?"

"Excuse me?" Obeying the unspoken summons, Corie scooted around Matt and peeked into the hidden nook.

In a circle of scorched asphalt where the snow had melted away sat what she assumed was her discarded iron skillet. A black stain of soot climbed the brick wall above it and surrounded the milk carton that had melted into a flat plank and sat in a pile of ash in the pan. More surviving bits of charred debris lay scattered around it, stretching out into the surrounding snow like bony fingers, as if someone had kicked snow onto the flames to put them out. She'd like to think this was a homeless person's fire that had gotten out of hand. But the fearful suspicion crawling up her spine told her that was just wishful thinking.

Corie hugged herself impossibly tighter, automatically defending her son—automatically throwing up every defensive barrier she possessed against the nightmares of her past. Another fire. Two in two days. Her voice came out brittle and sharp. "What are you implying?"

Matt adjusted his knit cap over his ears as if he was

making conversation about the weather. "I found a chemical residue coating both of the heating elements in the oven. I found the same gelatinous residue inside the lip of the milk carton."

"Why are you…?" Matt still wore his KCFD uniform and insulated jacket. He must have just come from work. Or maybe he was still on the clock. Corie backed away into the deeper snow across the alley, keeping both men in view. "Are you investigating me?"

Wally raised his gloved hands in a placating gesture. "Has your son been alone in the apartment today?"

Even worse.

"You're investigating Evan?" She shook her head, all her mama bear defensiveness welling inside her and making her shout. "He was at school or with me. All day long—until we got home a few minutes ago. I saw my oven was missing and came down to ask you about it. He's upstairs right now, getting ready for bed. But you're not going to interrogate him. He's a child. An innocent child."

Matt's tone remained calm, his stance annoyingly unaffected by her losing it like this. "I'm not accusing Evan of setting these fires with any malicious intent."

Semantics. An accusation was an accusation.

She glared at the building super. "*He* is."

Chapter Four

Katie Norwell remembered the flames shooting up into the night sky as Kenny torched their first home. A wailing toddler squirmed in her arms and tears streamed from her eyes to mingle with the blood at the corner of her mouth while her monster of a husband pinned her in front of him, her upper arms almost numb with the pinch of his grip.

As he forced her to watch his handiwork, Katie felt her entire future going up in flames. Kenny, on the other hand, seemed to be getting off on the destruction of the small house she had worked so hard to decorate and turn into a family home. "Insurance will pay for a bigger, brand-new home, more befitting my new position with the Corboni family."

She didn't bother arguing that she preferred history and character over modern ostentation. She didn't bother threatening to report his crime—unless she had a death wish. She was trapped, and he knew it. He smacked his lips as he whispered against her ear. "You're lucky I let you bring the boy out."

He didn't mean he'd done her a favor by letting

save their son. Danny would always be Kenny's prized possession. He meant she was lucky that he'd let her live.

"Corie?"

She snapped out of the memory at the firm, low-pitched call of her name.

Not Katie. She was Corie now.

That flash of memory belonged to the past. The wall of Matt Taylor standing in front of her, his dark eyes creased with concern, belonged to the present.

She rapidly blinked her surroundings into focus and gathered her thoughts. The remnants of two fires. Snow. Cold. She needed her coat. Kansas City. No Kenny. Bald man. Big man.

Corie tilted her gaze up to Matt's angular, darkly stubbled face.

He thought Evan had set these two small fires.

He didn't know what a real arsonist could do.

The hardness around his eyes softened when he sensed she recognized him and could be reasoned with again. "I don't mean Evan any harm. And I won't jump to any conclusions. I promise," Matt stated, making Mr. Stinson grumble about being accused of something himself and turning away. "I want the facts first."

"The facts are my son didn't set these fires." There was something about Matt's stoic demeanor that calmed her enough to speak rationally again. "Why would you think that?"

"Several things about them make me suspicious," Matt explained. Although she was certain he was wondering why she'd blown up like that, he was too polite to mention it. Or maybe her reaction made it look like she was hiding something. The hell of it was she was hiding a lot. "I asked Mr. Stinson if I could examine them. The signatures are too similar for me to think they were set by two different perps. The residue is what dripped into the pan and set your son's pizza on fire. The whole oven was primed to burn. If the detector hadn't gone off—if I hadn't smelled the smoke…"

She'd had nothing to put it out with beyond depriving the flames of oxygen. And she'd opened a window. This could have been a disaster. But surely not… There was no way this could be anything but a horrid coincidence, right? A chemical? The unfamiliar smell in her kitchen? A different sort of panic threatened to sink its talons into her. She stepped around Matt to confront the older man. "Mr. Stinson, was anyone besides you in my apartment today?"

"Just to move the oven out," he groused, clearly feeling underappreciated and defensive now that he was no longer the one asking questions. "I fixed the outlet, and Jeff helped me move the oven out on a dolly."

"Jeff? Who's Jeff?" She tried to picture the retired gentleman who'd fixed her garbage disposal last Thanksgiving when Wally had visited his daughter in Ohio. "I thought Phil somebody helped you."

"Phil remarried and moved to Arizona with his new wife. You probably don't know that because you're not around much," he added, as though working two jobs and spending her free time with her son were crimes instead of choices. "Jeff moved in about a month ago. Gets reduced rent as my new part-timer. He lives in the apartment right under yours—612. We were in and out of your place in half an hour."

Shouldn't that make her feel better, knowing no one had been in her apartment who couldn't be accounted for? Of course, she'd feel a lot better if she actually knew who this Jeff person was and could put a face to the name. There had to be another explanation for the fires, beyond the one that scared her more than anything else. She and Evan were safe. She had no proof that her past had caught up with them.

So, why did she feel like someone *had* violated her sanctuary?

Her shiver had nothing to do with the cold.

Matt was still calmly explaining his concerns in that deep, resonant voice. "According to my fire captain, it's a homemade fire starter usually used in vandalism. Spray or brush the flammable substance over the heating elements and crank the temperature until it ignites. Or drop a match into a milk jug filled with the incendiary compound."

She knew what he was implying. But he was wrong. Evan had been too young to know anything about his father's line of work—an arsonist for hire. All he remembered about Kenny Norwell was the yelling and the fist that had shattered her cheekbone when she picked up her toddler and drove away with nothing but the clothes on their backs. There were no tender memories— nothing but the fires and the hospital and the running and hiding until the rest of Kenny's crimes finally caught up with him. Once she'd given her testimony and the trial and sentencing were over, Katie Norwell had secured full custody of her son, cleared out her savings and sold her car, and gone to the judge to start a new life as Corie McGuire.

Logically, she knew that Matt had no idea about her past or Kenny's expertise—he wasn't making that connection. And she knew genetics didn't make Evan a firebug like his father had been. This had to be a sick joke. Yes, her son was obsessed with dragons. But that was a coping mechanism—to his child's brain, dragons were the strongest, most unbeatable creatures ever devised. A dragon would protect him against the monsters. A dragon controlled the flames—he wasn't consumed by them. Evan could not be fascinated by fire—she couldn't go through that kind of terror again. "You think Evan is responsible? He's eight years old. He doesn't know about flammable compounds, and he would never do anything risky like that to put himself in danger." She knew kids could be curious, but she also knew her son. In some ways, he was all sweet little child—but in one way, he was mature and protective beyond his years. "Evan would never do anything to put *me* in danger."

"I'm not accusing your son of anything malicious," Mr. Stinson insisted. "But part of my job is to make sure the tenants of this building stay safe. I know boys will be boys. And you can find out about anything on the internet these days."

"No." She was as emphatic as the chill in the air. "Evan did not set these fires."

Clearly both men believed they'd been deliberately set. Clearly, both men blamed her son. Both men were wrong.

Matt took a step toward her, and Corie flinched away. She glared up at him, and he retreated a step. His voice dropped to a husky timbre, probably meant to ease the import of whatever he was about to say. "Sometimes kids experiment with things that get out of hand and are more dangerous than they thought they would be. I've done some counseling with other kids who've pulled the fire alarm at school, for example. The fire department will go in and sit with the student and explain the importance of respecting their own safety and the safety of others—how answering false alarms could take us away from someone who truly needs our help."

She shoved a lock of loose hair behind her ear and held it there, creating another barrier between her and the world that wanted to attack the person she held most dear. "I'm familiar with that program. We've had firefighters come to our school and give that same talk." She glanced at the ruined oven and charred bricks. "But you're accusing my son of arson, not pulling a fire alarm on a dare or on a lark. Evan might have put a pizza in the oven, but he did not do this."

Matt glanced over at Mr. Stinson. The older man shrugged, as though he was biting his tongue on another possibility.

Corie saved him the trouble. "*I* didn't start that fire, either." She tipped her chin up to Matt, wondering if his concern was professional or personal, and wondering why the answer mattered to her. "My son doesn't need counseling. If these are arson fires, then someone else is responsible." She included the super in her warning.

"You've had a break-in in this building, and you need to step up security."

Wally Stinson clutched his coat in a dramatic gesture. "You think someone broke into this building and I don't know about it?"

Someone who'd washed his hands at her kitchen sink and wore a citrusy cologne.

Someone who shouldn't even know that Corie and Evan McGuire existed.

Suddenly, the wintry chill poured into her veins, chilling her from the inside out. "I have to go." She backed toward the door to the building. She needed to see her son. Now. "I'll pay for the stupid oven and clean up that mess myself."

"Mrs. McGuire, that's not what I'm saying," Mr. Stinson started. "You'll still get a new oven. I just wanted to make sure nothing else is gonna get damaged…"

Corie swiped her key and opened the door, hearing no more.

She hurried to the elevator. The doors opened the moment she pushed the call button. She had her finger on the seventh-floor button, and the doors were closing, when a big hand grabbed the door and pushed it open again.

Corie yelped and darted to the back of the elevator as Matt Taylor filled the opening. "I'm sorry."

"Sorry." She echoed his apology, hating that she'd screamed at her neighbor, who'd been nothing but kind to her and Evan. Until tonight. And even then, he'd been cautious in explaining his suspicions about her son playing with fire.

He stepped inside, sliding to the far corner of the elevator as the doors closed. As if a few feet of distance could make him any less imposing, or the scent of the cold, fresh air wafting off his uniform and jacket were any less enticing.

"I'm sorry," he apologized again. He pulled his stocking cap from his head and worked it between his hands before flattening his back against the side wall and adding a few extra inches of space between them. His gaze dropped to the death grip she held on the railing before those coffee-brown eyes settled on her wary, wide-eyed stare. "I know I'm a big, scary guy. I just wanted you to stop for a second and talk to me. Help me understand why you're upset—why you needed to run away."

They passed the second floor before she realized he was doing his damnedest to make himself as non-threatening as possible. Knowing he didn't deserve to be judged by Kenny Norwell's standards, Corie made a conscious effort to loosen her grip on the railing. She blinked, trying not to look so much like prey being eyed by a predator. "First, you are a big guy, yes. But you're not scary, Matt. You're gentle and kind, from what I can tell. You startled me, that's all. I'm…more skittish than the average woman. I own that."

"Why?"

His question surprised her. Most people politely kept their distance or dismissed her entirely when she went into escape mode. "There are no gray areas for you, are there? You have a question, you ask it. You see a thing that needs to be done, you do it." He waited. The elevator slowed as she hugged her arms around herself and gave him the briefest explanation possible. "My marriage to Evan's father was not a good one. I'm overly cautious around men as a result."

"He hurt you?"

"Kenny Norwell hurt a lot of people." The elevator doors opened, and Corie hurried down the hallway, aware that Matt was following her—and equally aware that he'd shortened his stride to maintain his distance. She appreciated his thoughtfulness, hated that she projected the air of a woman who needed that kind of kid-glove treatment and was rattled enough by the conversation in the alley that she unlocked her door and headed inside without looking back. "Excuse me. I need to see with my own eyes that Evan is okay."

"Why wouldn't he be—?" She closed the door on his question and quickly threw the dead bolt behind her. Her breath rushed out on a sigh full of regret as much as relief.

She didn't want to hurt Matt, but she was more used to guarding herself than being open, more used to being afraid than trusting. Corie listened for the sound of his key in his door before she fixed a smile on her face and headed back to Evan's room.

Peeking inside the doorway, she found him busy building his fortress again. "Hey, little man. Did you brush your teeth?"

Evan glanced up from his work to roll his eyes with the exhausted look of the downtrodden masses that only a small boy who'd lost precious playtime could manage. "For two whole minutes. It took forever."

Corie smiled, relieved to see he was fine, happy to hear his dramatic personality hadn't dimmed one iota and embarrassed to admit she owed the man across the hall an apology. "Get your book and climb under the covers. I need to talk to Mr. Taylor for a couple of minutes. I'll be right back."

"Okay. Tell Matt I said hi. And ask if he needs me to use his watch again. Maybe I could borrow it for school when we talk about technology." She arched an eyebrow and gave him the mom look. "Okay. Don't ask. I don't need a watch."

Oh, the drama. "To bed, mister."

"Yes, ma'am."

Once Evan was in bed and thumbing through the pages of his book, Corie slipped across the hall and knocked softly on Matt's door.

She curled her toes inside her sensible shoes, bracing herself for the door to swing open and the big man to suddenly fill the opening again. But he must have seen her through the peephole, because the door opened slowly and Matt leaned a shoulder against the door frame, trying and failing to look less imposing, and pleasing her all the more for making the effort.

He'd taken off his jacket and cap, rolled up the sleeves of his black uniform shirt and loosened a couple of buttons that gave her a tantalizing glimpse of another one of those T-shirts that hugged his muscular body so well. "Evan okay?"

"Yeah." Corie fiddled with the buttons of her own

sweater, feeling an unfamiliar stab of heat. She buried her hands in the pockets of her cardigan, hoping she hadn't looked like she was imagining undoing the rest of those buttons on his shirt. "Are you certain someone deliberately sabotaged my oven?"

Not the way she'd meant to start that apology.

But Matt didn't seem to mind. He nodded, one curt, certain nod that made her shiver again. "The fire in the alley was also deliberately set."

Just rip off the bandage and tell him.

"My ex-husband… He went to prison for arson—insurance fraud and witness intimidation. Sneaking into my apartment to destroy an appliance or tamper with a plug is the kind of thing he would have done… to harass me. To frighten me. He couldn't grasp that I wanted to end the marriage and sue for full custody of Evan." Matt's dark eyes never wavered from hers. He knew there was more to her story, but he didn't push her to spit it out. He waited patiently until she took in a deep breath and could say it. "My marriage was a lifetime ago. Kenny has spent most of the last six years in prison. He doesn't know where we live. He doesn't know his son. He doesn't know me. Not anymore."

She hugged her arms around her waist again, the momentary heat she'd felt fading as the past swept in. "I legally changed our names. Cut all ties to where we used to live. There's no way he could find me. He can't be responsible for this." She paused to take in the scope of his broad, inviting chest, wondering what he'd do if she threw herself against him. Wondering why the arms of a man—of Matt Taylor—seemed like refuge to her tonight. She hugged her sweater more tightly around herself instead, feeling it was a poor substitute for the heat and strength she could see in him. "Those two fires make me think the impossible. They make me worry." Corie pressed her fingers to her forehead, rubbing at the tension headache twisting there. "I want there to be another explanation besides Kenny tormenting us."

"If there is, I'll find it." Matt straightened to his full height but drifted back a step into his apartment. "Do I remind you of him?"

"Of Kenny?" Honestly, the only similarity that popped into her head was that they were both men. And Kenny hadn't even been very good at that. "No." She'd just confessed to making the stellar choice of marrying an abusive loser who set fires for a living and not being the woman Matt thought she was—and he was worried about scaring her? "You're half a foot taller than he is." And though they were both well-built men with dark hair, there was a difference about their brown eyes she wasn't sure she could explain. "His eyes are like a cold, empty void, and yours are…warm. Like a steaming cup of coffee." She allowed herself a few seconds to appreciate the heat shining from his eyes before shrugging off that fanciful notion. "Most importantly, your personalities are different. Kenny would never care that I was afraid of him. He wouldn't give me a chance to explain or defend myself. And he certainly would never apologize for startling me like you did."

Matt released a slow breath and nodded. "I can be pretty quiet. It's spooky when I don't say much."

"Spooky? Who told you that?"

"My brother Alex. And a woman I once dated."

"Well, Alex and what's-her-face are wrong. I think you just wait until you have the right thing to say." Although she could easily imagine Matt being a big, brooding presence if he ever got ticked off, he'd never shown her that side of him. "I bet there's a lot of thinking and decision making going on inside that head before you ever say a word. Maybe you're a little shy. And if that's so, I think it's sweet." She quickly put up her hand in apology. "And before you argue with me, *sweet* is a good thing."

"That's what my grandma says. If a woman calls one of us sweet, not to complain."

"I like your grandmother."

"She's one of a kind." The line of his mouth softened in what she hoped was his version of a smile.

The tension inside her skull eased a little. She liked being on good terms with Matt. She should end this conversation while she was ahead. She thumbed over her shoulder across the hall. "I'd better get inside. I promised Evan a bedtime story. We both have school in the morning, so…"

"Good night."

"Good night, Matt."

"Corie." She'd unlocked her door and pushed it partway open, but somehow he managed to stop her without touching her, without startling her. Corie turned as he braced one hand on the door frame beside her head, reversing their positions from a moment ago. "If I ever do anything that reminds you of your ex, you'll tell me, right? You won't just put up with it because you're a nice lady or you're worried about hurting my feelings or you think the truth will trigger my temper. It won't. I promise. You'll tell me to back off if I scare you?"

Kenny had rarely given her the option of pointing out when he was hurting or frightening her. If anything, he enjoyed it when she'd voiced her fears. It only made him want to torment her more, it seemed. Kenny had always needed to prove his strength, his power—and when the outside world hadn't let him be everything he wanted, he exerted that dominance over her. But Matt Taylor was a different sort of man than her ex had been. He knew he was strong, but he worked hard to play down his physicality instead of shoving it in her face. He was a little awkward, a little gruff—but he seemed like such a good man. A good neighbor. Maybe even a good friend. If she'd let him be.

Corie considered the earnestness of his request, then surprised herself almost as much as it must have surprised Matt when she reached for his hand down at his side and squeezed his fingers. "I will."

His hand was callused and warm and infinitely gentle as he folded his fingers around hers and squeezed back. "And I'll tell you the next time I investigate anything suspicious that relates to you or Evan."

She offered him an apologetic smile. "I'm super protective of my son. I overreacted."

"No. I overstepped my authority. Thought I recognized someone acting out the way I once did."

"You acted out?"

He rubbed the pad of his thumb across her knuckles in a gentle caress, but which of them he was soothing, she couldn't be sure, because the seriousness of his expression didn't change. "I started fires when I was a little boy. Younger than Evan, but still…" His grip pulsed lightly around hers. "Had some catastrophic consequences," he added without hinting at what that tragedy might have been. "I thought if Evan was dealing with something like that, I could help. Speak to him from experience."

"You played with fire?" That was an irony she understood far too well. "And yet you became a firefighter."

He nodded. "Atonement."

Atonement. That single raw word spoke volumes yet told her little. This gentle giant was a curious one. His honesty spoke to something deep inside her. His confession, whatever it might mean, lessened the embarrassment and caution she'd felt in revealing some of her own past. Her instinct was to comfort him. Her desire was to know him better. But instinct and desire hadn't served her very well in the past. Her brain told her to run far and fast from this connection she felt with Matt. But her heart was asking for something very different.

He pulled his hand from the door frame and brushed the back of his knuckles across her cheek. Her breath caught at the tender caress. But it wasn't fear of his touch that made her lips part as her skin suffused with heat. "I want you and Evan to be safe."

Corie realized they'd been holding hands this whole time. Their eyes had been locked together, and she hadn't once felt the need to bolt. But maybe she'd be smart to at least walk away. She reached up to pull his fingers from her face and grasped each of his hands between them. "Thank you for caring, Matt. But I got this."

He nodded. "Remember what I said. Be honest with me. And if anything—anyone—makes you afraid again—"

"I'll call 9-1-1 and ask for the firefighter next door."

"You could just call my number. Here." He was the one who was finally strong enough to release their hold on each other to pull his billfold from his back pocket. He handed her a KCFD business card with his name and both his cell and the firehouse numbers on it.

"Lieutenant Taylor. Impressive." She hugged the information to her chest. "Thank you. Good night, Matt."

"Good night, Corie. Tell Evan good-night, too. I'll wait 'til you lock the dead bolt behind you."

Once she'd locked her door, Corie leaned back against it. She smiled when she heard his door close and lock across the hall. Was he always this true to his word? Did Matt show this kind of caring to everyone?

They'd held hands longer than a simple thank-you called for. Corie raised her hand in front of her face and marveled at the sensations of warmth and caring still prickling in her fingers from where Matt's big, callused hand had folded so gently around hers. Then she brushed her fingers across her cheek. She hadn't cared about a man's touch in years. But tonight, she'd actually enjoyed that simple, caring contact. She drew her fingertips across her lips, wondering if his mouth would be equally gentle pressed against hers. Or would his kiss be more demanding, as befitted his size and strength? Her pulse beat with intensified interest, and her body flushed with a long-forgotten warmth. Did she even have it in her to respond to real, raw passion like that anymore? If the memory of Matt's touch still lingered on her skin, what would it feel like if her whole body was wrapped up against his?

The heat she felt deepened and spread through her body, triggering a deliciously female response to sensations she could only imagine. Her womanly responses to men had lain dormant for so long. Once, she'd shut them down to protect at least a part of herself from Kenny, and she'd never felt compelled to resurrect that sweet tingling of normal desire in her breasts and womb. She'd never been brave enough to indulge that silky heaviness that warmed her from the inside out. Matt Taylor wasn't classically handsome, and he had no smooth charm that she could detect. But there was no denying his utter masculinity, or her basic feminine response to all that maleness. He was an unexpected temptation to her rusty hormones. He was interesting. A little mysterious and seriously hot. She was tempted to get to know him better—to do much more than simply hold his hand and share a hushed conversation at her apartment door.

"Mo-om!"

Perfect timing. Evan drew out her name on two syllables, pulling her back to reality and quashing any momentary fantasy she had about Matt. She tucked his card into the pocket of her sweater and pushed away from the door. If she wasn't careful, she was going to develop a crush on the firefighter next door. Maybe she already had.

But she had a family to support, a college degree to

earn, and an eight-year-old son who needed story time and some cuddling before he'd go to sleep.

Corie didn't have time to indulge in whatever her hormones or heart were trying to tell her about Matt Taylor.

Chapter Five

After the second rapid knock on his door, Matt pulled his jeans down over his work boots and hurried out of the bedroom, tucking in his insulated undershirt and shrugging on a flannel shirt as he strode through his apartment. "Coming!" he barked.

He peered through the peephole to see which of his brothers had stopped by to tell him to hustle his butt over to Grandma Martha's old condo, where they were converging tonight to continue the remodeling and repair work needed before putting it on the market in the spring or summer. But there was no annoying brother out there. His nostrils flared as he dragged in a steadying breath to tamp down the mix of concern and anticipation surging inside him before he quietly opened the door to the blonde and her young son standing in the hallway.

"What's wrong?" he asked, reading the harried expression on Corie McGuire's face.

She hugged Evan back against her stomach and retreated half a step, possibly rethinking knocking on the Big Bad Wolf's door. "Is this a bad time?"

"For what?" He buttoned his shirt and straightened the collar, waiting for an explanation.

Corie nodded, deciding the reason for being here was more important than whatever second-guessing was playing through her head right now. "I have a big favor to ask you. I don't know if I have the right…" Not an emergency. The wariness in him eased a fraction, and he rolled up his sleeves while Corie spewed out a stream of disconnected sentences. "I got called in to work this evening. One of the girls went home sick. It's a chance to pick up a few extra hours. But it means working until closing, and it's a school night for Evan." She paused for breath. Nope. He still didn't understand what she needed from him. "I know it's impossibly short notice, but I heard you come home from work a few minutes ago, and… I'm not giving you much time to relax, but would you be able to watch Evan for me this evening?"

He needed clarity. Was she in a panic caused by time constraints? Or was he missing something more serious here? He glanced down at Evan and the green, purple and yellow plastic dragon he carried. "Babysit?"

Evan's lips buzzed with a groany sigh as he pushed away from his mother. "I'm not a baby."

The boy was put out, not in distress. This didn't sound too serious. Maybe Corie was uncomfortable asking for a favor. Maybe she was uncomfortable asking *him* for a favor. Maybe she felt like she was out of options and he was the last resort. The poor choice he'd made watching his little brother, Mark, twenty-six years ago had never been repeated. He might not be the fun uncle, but in the years since, he'd been trusted with younger cousins and nieces and nephews, and they'd all survived. In his experience, you kept the kid busy, fed him and put him to bed on time, and he'd never had an issue. If she needed a sitter, he was her man. How could he make this easier for her?

Maybe she wasn't the one he needed to make friends with.

Matt leaned against the door frame and hunched his posture a tad, turning his focus down to the green-eyed boy and trying to sound like…not the Big Bad Wolf. "Poor choice of words, Ev. My apologies. You and your dragon buddy want to hang out for a while?" He was still looking down when he raised his gaze to Corie's. "His regular sitter isn't available?"

Color blossomed in her cheeks. "Regular? Um… I don't have anyone on speed dial—"

"Usually I go with Mom to the diner," Evan volunteered, innocently unaware of his mother's embarrassment as he matter-of-factly explained their predicament. "But that's when she works the afternoon shift after school. I can only go on Fridays and Saturdays when she closes. She calls me a growly butt in the morning if I stay up too late. And staying up until the diner closes means *too late*."

Understanding dawned. Corie didn't have a regular sitter. They went to school together in the morning, and he went to campus with her when she had classes and to Pearl's Diner when she had to work. And she'd just mentioned the need to pick up extra hours, so paying for an emergency sitter might not be an option for her.

He was trained to handle emergencies—large

or about the size of a small eight-year-old boy. Matt dropped his gaze to Evan again. "Can you handle a hammer?"

Evan screwed his lightly freckled face up in a suspicious frown. "I don't know."

Matt held up a finger, warning mother and son not to leave as he dashed into the spare bedroom to pull his toolbox from the closet and retrieve a hammer. He came back to the door and found both mother and son peeking into his apartment, with Corie clinging to Evan's shoulders to keep him from following Matt inside. He wouldn't have minded the boy traipsing along behind him. "Let me show you." Matt knelt in front of Evan, trading the hammer for the dragon, letting the boy feel the weight of the tool and watching how he grabbed it with both hands in the middle. Matt moved Evan's hand to the proper position and demonstrated an easy swing. "Did anybody ever teach you to hold the handle near the end, and not up by the peen?"

"Peen?" Evan giggled, no doubt thinking that was the past tense of another word. Matt had been a boy once, too. "That's not a real word."

"The peen is the heavy metal part of the hammer that you hit the nail with."

"It is? I thought you were talking about…" His mouth rounded with an O of excitement before tilting his face up to Corie. "Mom, can I try? I want to hammer a nail."

Corie frowned. "Are you working on a project? I don't want him to get in your way."

"He won't." Matt stood, firmly grasping the hammer to stop Evan from swinging it. He had a feeling it wouldn't be too hard to keep this kid entertained. "Is it all right if I take him to my grandmother's old apartment a few blocks from here? I planned to meet my brothers to work on renovations. I'll make sure Evan's buckled into the back seat of my truck. I'm a safe driver. I drive the fire engine. Never had an accident."

"You drive the fire engine?" Evan's eager response told her that was about the coolest thing he'd ever heard. Way cooler than even the chance to hammer on something. No way was Corie going to be able to say no without disappointing her son. Or Matt. Besides, there was no need for her to. Everyone else would be showing up at his grandma's apartment with a spouse or fiancée, children and probably a dog. Matt liked the idea of bringing his own sidekick to the party. "Can I drive it?"

"You're a little young for that, bud." Matt eased his no by ruffling his fingers through Evan's soft, staticky hair. It was funny how some of the longer strands stuck straight out or up. Evan McGuire might be a curious, sheltered kid, but he was all boy. "I'll show you my Lucky 13 truck sometime. You can climb inside, sit behind the wheel. But that's another outing. And we're not going anywhere tonight unless your mom says it's okay."

"Mom, pleee-a-ssse! He drives the fire engine and I can hammer." He hoped the kid went into music, because he could draw a word out across several different notes.

Corie shook her head, looking like she'd already lost the battle. "You're sure he won't be in your way?"

"Positive."

Corie's blond ponytail bobbed across her shoulders as she shook her head, surrendering to the boy jumping up and down between them. "You'll have him home by bedtime?"

"He'll be snoring when you get home from work."

Evan finally stopped his bouncing. "Hey, I don't snore. But, can I, Mom? Please? I want to learn about peens." He beamed a gap-toothed grin, as though saying the word out loud made him want to laugh again. "And fire engines." Evan tugged on Matt's sleeve. "Will you tell me about your fire engine?"

"You bet." Matt tucked the hammer through his belt and rested a hand on Evan's shoulder before he started that bouncing thing again.

Corie tilted her soft green eyes up at Matt, and he couldn't look away. "You'll keep him away from any power tools?"

"Mo-om!"

"My brother Mark is a registered EMT, and my first aid training is current. If he gets hurt, we'll fix him."

"If he gets hurt—?"

"He won't get hurt."

Her soft green eyes rolled heavenward, and he thought he detected the hint of a laugh. "Sometimes I can't tell when you're joking. I have to get used to that dry sense of humor." Matt felt his mouth relaxing into an answering smile. *Getting used to* would require spending more time together. He liked that idea. "Okay. To all of it." She combed her fingers through Evan's hair, trying to neaten it up a tad before she cupped his face in her hands. "Homework done?"

"Yep."

She arched a suspicious eyebrow, and Evan groaned again.

"I still have multiplication tables."

"Run and get your coat and backpack. You'll finish the math before you help Matt and his brothers, okay?"

"Okay." Evan was darting across the hall and tearing through their apartment before Corie finished her question.

Unlike her son's flyaway hair, Corie's hung thick and straight. She brushed a loose strand of it off her cheek and tucked it behind her ear. Matt's fingers tingled with the urge to do the job for her. And linger. And maybe free that ponytail to see how long her hair was when it fell loose and straight. "I hope you know what you're getting into."

Matt curled his hands into his fists and tore his thoughts away from sifting her thick, shiny hair though his fingers. "I think I can handle second grade math."

"Yes, but can you handle a second grader?"

Although he suspected she was teasing him as much as giving fair warning, Matt felt compelled to reassure her. "I'll have help. My grandmother and sisters-in-law are bringing food. There'll be plenty for him to eat. My brother Pike will bring his son. Gideon Jr. is close to Evan's age. He'll be fine."

"Okay. Thank you." Corie seemed pleased with his explanation, if a little overwhelmed by the loving, crowded scene he'd described. "I'll owe you a whole pie for helping me out tonight."

"You'll owe me nothing."

She smiled—a huge, beautiful, bright curve that gave him a glimpse of straight, white teeth and softened the tension around her lips. Didn't she understand that smile was payment enough?

"I'll bring the pie, anyway." When she reached out to squeeze his hand, Matt squeezed back. He loved the feel of her hand in his. Small and soft compared to his big workingman's hands, but strong. With sensible, unadorned nails and the faded stripe of a scar between her thumb and forefinger. Her fingers tightened around his before she released him and backed across the hallway into her apartment. "I'd better get changed. And I won't forget the pie!"

Chapter Six

Three hours later, Matt raised his hands in triumph as he busted through the kitchen wall they were taking down with their fire axes a split second before his younger brother, Mark, broke through the drywall in his section. His older brothers, Alex and Pike, slapped him on the shoulder and congratulated him before razzing Mark.

"That's how you swing an ax." Pike smacked Matt on the shoulder.

Alex agreed. "Told you he'd win."

"Not fair," Mark protested, always ready to prove himself against any of his three older brothers. "Matt's arms are a good two inches longer than mine."

"Why do you think I didn't take that bet?" Alex, the oldest and shortest of the four, teased.

Pike Taylor, the only brother with blond hair, picked up a couple of pieces of Sheetrock and carried them to the trash can in the dining room that was now open to the kitchen, save for the two-by-four framework that was coming down next. "If you don't want to give Matt credit, think of it this way—Alex and I are the real winners because we didn't have to do any of the teardown work." He glanced down at Alex, who was picking up the debris Matt and Mark had created. "Right, Shrimp?"

"Really? Shrimp?" Alex tossed his load in after Pike's. "I always thought it was you and me against the wonder twins."

"Un-uh," Mark reminded him, poking Matt in the chest. "He's two years older than I am. I'm the beloved baby boy. Grandma said so. It's every man for himself in this family."

"Matt!" Evan shot around the corner and skidded to a halt when he saw the four men laughing and ribbing each other. The dragon he carried had sprouted a second set of yellow wings, telling Matt how Evan and his nephew Gideon were staying busy. The boy's wide-eyed gaze settled on the long-handled ax cradled across Matt's shoulders. "Where's your hammer? Are you okay? Did you cut yourself?"

Matt questioned the pale tinge beneath Evan's brown freckles. "I'm fine, bud."

"Do you dragon swear?"

Um, yeah?

"What are you boys arguing about now?" Meghan Taylor, the brothers' adoptive mother, showed nary a wrinkle on her youthful features, except for the amusement crinkling beside her honey-brown eyes, when she appeared behind Evan. She carried a toddler wearing pink, fuzzy pajamas in one arm, and rested her free hand on Evan's shoulder as they peeked around the corner from the bedrooms, where she and their father, Gideon Sr., were corralling Evan, Pike's son, Gideon Jr., and Pike's little girl, Dorie. "Seriously? You two used your regulation axes to take down that wall? It's a good thing that no one lives above or below Martha's apartment with the fuss you four are making."

Matt's gaze zeroed in on Evan's pale features as the boy shrank back against Matt's mother. Had the kid been startled by the pounding and crashing? Did the potential weapon he wielded make the boy think he and Mark had attacked more than the wall? "It's a noisy job, Ev," he explained, lowering the ax to cradle it securely between both hands. "We're all good here." He wasn't sure of the protocol, but he drew a cross over his heart. "I dragon swear."

Mark set his ax in a safe corner and threw up his hands. "Speak for yourself, big guy. Mom, you know these three bullied me into turning this into a race."

"Un-uh." Their mother had heard—and dismissed—that excuse many times over the years. "The axes were probably your idea."

"I told them breaking through the wall like that could be dangerous and wanted no part of it." Pike was the next to offer up an explanation, as he swooped in to pluck Dorie from their mother's arms and blow a raspberry onto his daughter's cheek, making the tiny blonde giggle with delight. Evan tilted his chin up, looking more curious than alarmed by the farting sound and resulting laughter. "Can I help it if they won't listen to reason?"

Matt was pleased to see his mother switch both hands to Evan's shoulders, perhaps sensing the boy's nervousness at being surrounded by all this noise and activity.

"How hard did you try?" Meghan asked Pike with a deadpan tone of doubt.

"Not as hard as I did," Alex insisted, tossing more debris into the trash. "That's what sledgehammers are for, I said. But have these three yahoos ever listened to me?"

Their mother shook her head, then turned her soft brown eyes up to Matt. "You're my last hope for a straight answer, son. Why would you all risk someone getting hurt and making all this racket by chopping through walls?"

"The job needed to be done." Matt might have learned that deadpan delivery from his mom. "Since it's an exercise we practice time and again in our firefighter training, I knew we could do it safely."

"And we have a winner." Meghan Taylor bent down and whispered a reassurance against Evan's ear. "I told you they were fine. Matt just beat all his brothers in the wall-chopping competition."

As their mother beamed him a smile, Matt was instantly struck by the reminder of how good it felt to be the one who could make someone he cared about light up like that. Maybe that's why Corie's smile was such a turn-on. It was rare and hard-won. And though he was probably a fool for thinking it, her smile felt like it was a special gift just for him.

While the quiet moment passed between mother and son, there was laughter and a round of applause from their grandmother, Pike's wife, Hope, Alex's wife, Audrey, and Mark's fiancée, Amy, as they joined them. The younger women were supposed to be painting the walls and trim in the living room. But the "Yay, Matt!" from Evan was the only voice of approval he needed to hear. Whatever concerns the boy had had when he'd run out to the main room disappeared with Meghan's explanation. When Matt caught Evan's gaze across the room and winked at him, the boy flashed his gap-toothed grin and dashed back into the bedroom to play.

Yep. Making someone smile felt pretty damn special.

As he had many times throughout his life, Matt thanked the fates that had landed him in this family. The competition was real, and occasionally intense, but always full of love. And the ringleader of them all—a shrinking, widowed, eighty-four-year-old woman— quieted the room by simply raising a plastic tub filled with cookies she'd baked to go with the dinner they'd all eaten earlier. Martha Taylor swatted aside Pike's hand as he reached for a cookie. She wrapped her arthritic fingers around Matt's forearm and held on to him for balance as she stepped around the debris.

"The first snickerdoodle is for our winner," she announced, handing Matt one of her delicious cookies. He promptly stuffed it whole into his mouth while she hugged him around the waist. He dropped a kiss to the top of her snow-white hair before she pulled away and handed an equally delicious cookie to Mark. "And a consolation prize for second place."

"We always try harder." Mark held his cookie up and did a misplaced victory dance before kissing Martha's weathered cheek and hugging her, too. "Thanks, Grandma."

"What about the rest of us?" Alex pouted, drawing his red-haired wife, Audrey, to his side. "I'm starving."

Audrey poked him in the flank. "You had seconds at dinner."

"Yeah, but they weren't cookies."

"Oh, all right," Martha relented, as they'd all known she would. "Time for us all to take a break. Everybody dig in." She wrapped a stack of cookies in a paper napkin and handed them to Pike's shy wife, Hope, who'd been rubbing noses with Dorie and brushing crumbs from Pike's chin. "Take some for Evan and the Gideons."

"I'd be happy to."

"I'll help," Pike offered.

Before they headed down the hallway, Hope swiped her fingers across Pike's lips, even though the crumbs on his face were long gone. When they lingered there a second and Pike's blue eyes heated at the contact, Matt felt a spike of envy. Not because he lusted after his sister-in-law or begrudged his brother his well-earned happiness, but because he wanted that, too—that connection with a woman who had eyes only for him. He wanted that connection with Corie McGuire.

Only, he wasn't quite sure how to make that happen. Or if Corie was even interested in him trying.

He was thirty years old and had never been in a serious relationship. He'd dated. He'd had sex. But nothing had ever worked out for him. Probably something to do with being six foot five and what that one blind date his brothers had set him up with had described as *spooky quiet*. He didn't always have a lot to say and got stuck in his head sometimes while he thought things through before he did speak. He lacked Mark's glib sense of humor and Alex's outgoing personality. Even Pike had a goofy sort of nerd charm going for him. Matt was just… Matt. Physical. Direct. He'd been a troubled kid who didn't speak for months after his birth parents' deaths—not until Meghan and Gideon Taylor had done their patient, loving child-whisperer thing with him and gotten him to open up about the tragedy he felt responsible for. And though he'd worked through his demons, it was still hard for him not to be that guarded, excessively observant survivor he'd once been.

Yep. A relationship with him probably wasn't for the faint of heart.

The man who had saved Matt's life when he'd been that silent little boy, Gideon Taylor Sr., strode into the main room, sliding his arm around Meghan's waist, unknowingly completing the image that everyone in this family had a partner except for Matt…and his widowed grandmother. But she'd been blessed to have been married to their grandfather Sid for more than sixty years, until his death this past summer. "None of the cookies made it past those two boys and Pike." His dad pointed to each of his three remaining sons around the room. "Talk about déjà vu." But he was grinning. "Ma, you got any more?"

Martha held out the tub for him to help himself to a snickerdoodle. "I'm so fortunate that you're all helping me with this remodeling project. I love how you've opened the kitchen up to the rest of the apartment. Makes me sorry that I had to move." She put up a hand before Gideon could remind her of her health issues and the flight of stairs leading to the front door, which was no longer safe for her to negotiate on her own. "I know it's for the best, and I admit I'm having fun finding the perfect place to put everything in my new home. But do you know how many years I was stuck back in that kitchen cooking, missing out on all the activity out here?"

"We were all in the kitchen with you, Ma." Gideon dropped an arm around her shoulders. "You never missed a thing." She leaned into the kiss he pressed to her temple. "Come on. Let's get back to my grandkids and your great-grands and stay out of harm's way while the boys finish tearing down in here." It wasn't hard for him to reach around Martha and pluck a second cookie to munch on. "And bring these with you so the big boys don't eat them all."

Martha might be in her eighties, but she was quick. She ducked from beneath her son's arm and faced the middle generation of young men who had torn up her kitchen. "But I want to hear about Matthew's young woman."

"Oh?" Gideon and Meghan stopped and turned, both looking at Matt with hope and curiosity. Great. Now his parents would be part of the inquisition, too. "You're seeing someone?" his dad asked.

Matt carried his ax to his toolbox and slipped the protective cover over the sharp blade. Then he picked up a broom and dustpan to attack the powdery drywall dust on the floor, hoping the personal question would just go away.

"Evan's mother," Martha offered when Matt didn't immediately respond.

"We're not *seeing* each other," Matt clarified for his father. "Corie and I are friends."

His brothers and sisters-in-law filled the room with teasing catcalls. His father slowly munched his cookie, his narrowed eyes assessing the full disclosure or lack thereof in Matt's response. Gideon Taylor had earned the silvered hair at his temples after raising the four of them. He knew how to wait out his sons until he got the answer he wanted.

And though Matt had gone back to work, his younger brother, Mark, ignored the shushing from his fiancée and poked the bull. "Tell us what she looks like, Matt."

Matt focused on the muscles in his arms and hands as he worked, trying to ignore his well-meaning family. Sweep. Dump. Sweep some more. But it seemed everyone was waiting for his answer now. "Prettier than you."

"Impossible." Amy swatted Mark's shoulder at that joking remark, but his baby bro wouldn't let the subject drop. Instead, Mark pulled the trash can closer, and he and Alex helped Matt with the cleanup job. "Just trying to get a sense of who's rockin' your world, big brother. Does Evan take after her?"

Although he knew everybody in the room was hanging on the details he wasn't sure he should share, Matt couldn't help but picture his pretty neighbor. "Same mossy-green eyes." He mentally compared her image to Evan—a cautious, curious boy who didn't know whether to be the man of the house or Corie's baby boy. "Corie doesn't have freckles like Evan. Her hair's the color of a ripe wheat field."

Alex paused with the remains of a shattered two-by-four in each hand. "A ripe wheat field? When did you become a poet?"

As Alex stuffed the boards into the trash, Mark continued the interrogation. "Is she the reason you were asking Captain Redding about old-school fire starters?"

Alex pulled out his phone. "That reminds me. I did a rundown on that name you asked me about—Kenneth Norwell. Career criminal with a long rap sheet." As much as he knew mentioning the word *criminal* while talking about Corie and Evan would only make his family more curious to learn about them, Matt mentally logged the information Alex was reading off his phone. "His current address is Jefferson City. Apparently, he didn't move too far from the penitentiary once he got out. He hasn't missed a check-in with his parole officer there—met with him last week. There's no indication of him living or working here in KC."

It was no surprise that their father was going to let mention of a paroled prisoner slide. "Why do you have KCPD checking the status of a paroled prisoner?" Gideon asked. "And why are you talking to Kyle Redding about incendiaries?"

Matt supposed if he had more of a social life, his interest in helping Corie and Evan wouldn't be such big news with his family tonight. "There was an oven fire at Corie's place. I made sure it was out. Another fire the next night in the alley behind the building. Something about them seemed hinky, so I was following up on my hunch."

"Arson?" his father asked. As chief arson investigator for the KCFD, Gideon Taylor Sr. certainly knew his way around a fire—probably better than any of them, except their mother, who was captain at another firehouse.

Matt nodded. "Corie insists that Evan wouldn't mess with anything like that and that he knows all about fire safety. But if it wasn't either of them, then somebody was in their apartment. Coated the heating elements with a flammable substance. Used it again in the alley fire."

Gideon's dark eyes narrowed with suspicion. "I don't like the sound of that."

Amy hugged her arms around her waist and shivered. "Arson fires are about the scariest thing I've ever had to deal with." She looked across the room to Mark, who was already crossing toward her. They'd both barely survived the work of an arsonist this past summer. "I'd still have a home, and Gran and I wouldn't be living with this guy."

Mark hugged her close. "You *like* living with this guy."

"I do." Amy nestled her forehead at the juncture of Mark's neck and shoulder. "And marrying him."

"And marrying him." She reached up to touch his face, and the unbreakable bond the two of them shared gave her the courage to smile before turning to face the rest of them. "So, big, bad Matt rescued Corie from a fire in her kitchen. Is that what all you Taylor boys do? Rescue the women you love?"

Love? Um...

Mark rubbed his hands up and down her arms, still soothing away the nightmare they'd survived. "Red, you said you don't like to be rescued."

"Well, I don't always like it because I'm a stubbornly independent woman, and I believe I can take care of myself," she teased. "But it *is* hot."

She looked to Audrey, who linked her arm with Alex's and nodded. "Super hot. It means the world to know someone's got your back and you can trust him without reservation. It allows us to be as strong as we need to be."

Alex turned and pressed a kiss to her forehead. "That little girl we're adopting will be lucky to have you for her mama."

Why couldn't his family discuss the weather or how much they missed Royals baseball like other, normal Kansas Citians?

Matt loved Amy like a sister and believed Mark had found a treasure, but the woman had no trouble speaking her mind. "Matt's hot. I bet Corie's hot, too."

Mark's cheeks turned a pale shade of pink that matched the embarrassment Matt felt at her compliment. "Could we stop saying hot? Unless you're referring to me?"

"Oh, you know how I like to refer to you, Fire Man."

Although he was grinning, Gideon shook his head as the subtext between the newly engaged couple's banter. "Hello, you two—you have an audience—and children in the next room. Save it for after the wedding."

"Did I miss something? Who's hot?" Meghan re-entered the room to stand beside her husband. "Matthew's girlfriend?"

"Mom, no. I don't have a girl… Corie is a friend. I'm just watching Evan while she's at work tonight."

"And investigating some mysterious circumstances surrounding her," Gideon added, his tone laced with concern. "Sounds like you're pretty involved to me, son."

"I like to know what I'm dealing with," Matt insisted. "And if Evan has anything to do with those fires, if he's trying to emulate his father or he's crying out for attention because the creep chose a life of crime over him, then—"

"You're the best man to help him." Probably better than anyone here, his mother understood just how far he had come since he'd been the troubled little boy who'd set the fire that had killed his birth parents. "Other than being a little skittish around all of us—and who wouldn't be?—I'm not seeing any indication that he's withdrawn or hiding something."

"Evan seems like a pretty cool kid to me," Pike added as he rejoined them. "He's making sure Junior and Dorie stay safe and share their cookies, even though Mom and Dad and Hope have been in there with them most of the evening. And that castle they're building is pretty sweet. The kid's going to be an architect one day."

Or was there something so frightening in his real life that he felt he had to keep building imaginary fortresses to feel safe?

Pike crossed the room to join them in picking up

the mess they'd made. "So, we're talking about Evan's mom? Is she the one who finally woke up Matt here?"

Alex helped him move the bank of old cabinets they'd taken apart to the side of the kitchen. "She has hair like a 'ripe wheat field.' Quote, unquote."

"When did you become a poet?" Pike echoed Alex's earlier question. Apparently, Matt's factual description of Corie's hair had revealed something he hadn't intended to. "This sounds serious."

Matt realized he was surrounded on all sides and commanding way too much attention. "Don't any of you have work to do?"

Martha Taylor had an answer for him. "I don't. Certainly, nothing as interesting as this conversation."

"Grandma!"

Fortunately, his mother had always been his strongest ally. "Give it a rest, boys." From the time they'd first met in the foster home where they'd all been living, Matt, Mark, Alex and Pike had been Meghan Taylor's boys. Becoming adults hadn't changed the nickname or the bond. She reached up to cup Matt's cheek and smiled. "I know you've just been waiting for the right one to come along. I'd like to meet Corie sometime. I hope she knows what a treasure you are." Then she added, in a soft whisper for his ears alone, "I hope you know, too." As she pulled away, she added, "And remember, firefighters work as a team. If there is something dangerous around Evan and his mother, you don't take it on alone." Her look encompassed the entire room. "You have allies."

"Yes, ma'am."

Despite the dramatic sigh of disappointment from Grandma Martha, the spotlight on Matt finally faded. The younger women returned to their painting as Gideon walked his wife and mother down the hall to watch the children. Matt and his brothers got to work on the last of the cleanup and prepping the expanded kitchen for the work they were going to do this weekend.

However, Mark, in all his newly engaged happiness, wouldn't let it go. He knocked loose the remaining dangling bits of drywall and tossed the biggest piece at Matt. "They say when the big ones fall, they fall hard."

Matt caught the piece squarely against his chest and shoved it into the trash. "Give it a rest, Mark."

Evan popped in again, his mouth wrinkled with concern as he eyed the dusty residue clinging to Matt's dark flannel shirt. The kid must have some kind of danger radar. Or he was more of a worrywart than anyone his age should be. "Matt, did you fall? Are you hurt?"

As worried about Evan's paranoia as he was glad for the reprieve from Let's Pick Apart Matt's Love Life Night, Matt scooped him up in his arms and rested the boy on his hip. "I'm fine, bud. You know, in many ways, you're lucky you're an only child."

"Huh?"

Matt was already striding from the room. He'd done most of the heavy lifting tonight. Let his annoying brothers handle the rest of the cleanup. "Show me this castle you and Gid are building."

Evan's arm rested lightly on Matt's shoulder, seeming to like being able to look him straight in the eye. "Can I hammer something again?"

Matt paused at the entrance to the hallway and looked back at his brothers. "Sure. I've got a trio of numbskulls you can start with…" Matt veed two fingers toward his eyes, then pointed to Mark, Pike and Alex, indicating he'd be watching them for any more teasing…and would put a stop to it when they didn't have an audience that included an impressionable child or their delicate grandmother. Alex laughed. Pike nodded, conceding that Matt was leaving with the upper hand. Mark threw his hands up in protest, as if affronted. So much love and support. So much a pain in the—

"What's a numbskull?" Evan asked.

Matt shook his head as his brothers laughed behind him. He needed to think about how he was going to explain that one to an eight-year-old.

By the end of another hour, the kitchen was prepped for new cabinets and tile. Paint cans had been sealed, dust had been swept up, his family had given the state of his love life a temporary rest, and Matt was walking Evan down the steps to the sidewalk in front of his grandmother's condo. "This way, bud." Evan kicked up puffs of snow as he shuffled along beside Matt. "I promised your mom I'd have you in bed by nine o'clock, so we'd better hustle."

"I'm not sleepy," he protested through his wide yawn.

Matt bit back his grin. "I know. If you want to close your eyes and rest for a few minutes on the drive home, that'd be okay."

"Can I come help again? Grandma Martha said she'd

bake chocolate chip cookies next time. They're my favorite. She said to call her Grandma Martha because I was a nice boy, and I was helping her, even though she's not my real grandma." Since Matt's hands were full with his ax and toolbox, Evan tugged on the sleeve of his coat to stop him. "I don't have a real grandma. Is it okay if I share yours?"

This kid worried way too much about other people's feelings and safety for someone his age. Not for the first time this evening, Matt wondered what events had shaped his young life. Corie had confessed that her ex had *hurt a lot of people*. Anger burned through Matt's blood at the idea that any of that violence might have touched Evan.

"If she said it's okay, then it's fine by me." He set his tools down on the sidewalk beside his truck and lifted Evan into the bed of the pickup so the boy could help him stow his ax and toolbox in the metal cargo box behind the cab.

Matt thought he heard the scrape of footsteps on the sidewalk. But with Evan's boots raising a muffled metallic sound in the bed of his truck, he couldn't isolate the noise. He glanced behind him to see if one of his brothers had followed them out. But the circle of illumination from the streetlamp in front of the old butcher shop was empty. A glance up the block revealed no pedestrians, either. Sometimes these tall brick and limestone buildings lining either side of the street in the City Market district captured sound and reflected it back off the hard surfaces, especially on a clear, cold night like this with little wind to dampen the echoing sounds.

Of course, there were shadows at the fringes of every streetlight and in the alleyways between buildings. And with vehicles parked along the curbs, someone hunched against the cold might not be readily visible. Matt pushed up the edges of his knit cap and trained his ears to try and pinpoint the company he couldn't see. But with Evan rattling Matt's toolbox as the boy insisted on lifting it himself, as well as his ongoing commentary about all things construction and cookie related, it was pretty impossible to hear anything else.

Probably his overtaxed sense of alertness, anyway. If he had heard the last steps of someone scurrying inside a warm building, there wasn't any real need to be concerned. This might once have been a decaying working-class neighborhood, but it had enjoyed a rebirth of tourism and an influx of professionals and young families who both lived and worked closer to the heart of the city. This wasn't a particularly dangerous neighborhood. Getting Evan out of this single-degree weather was probably a more pressing concern.

"Come on, bud." Once Evan had closed the lid and locked it, Matt helped him jump down and climb up into the back seat of his crew cab. Matt buckled him in, then ruffled the bangs that stuck out from beneath Evan's stocking cap. "Did you have fun tonight?"

"I like hammering, but can I use your ax next time?"

"Probably not the ax. It's heavy and it's dangerous. But we'll see about putting a paintbrush in your hands." There was still plenty of work to do on the condo above his late grandfather's butcher shop. Once they finished the remodel, they could sell it for a nice enough price that Grandma Martha could pay off the single-story ranch home she'd moved into that summer. The question was, would Corie be willing to trust Evan with him again? Once he mentioned axes and the fact he'd asked his brother to run a check on Evan's father, she might reconsider. "It'll be up to your mom."

"Cool." The smile Evan flashed was missing two full teeth, but it hit Matt with the same intensity that Corie's smile had.

Good grief. Maybe his family was seeing something in him that Matt hadn't fully admitted yet—he was falling for the family next door—not just the pretty mom whose smile and touch could set him off-kilter, but the little boy who seemed haunted by some of the same shadows Matt remembered from his own early childhood. The McGuires needed him. Or maybe they just needed someone—and he wanted to volunteer for the job.

Matt closed the rear door and stepped out into the street to walk around to the driver's side. But a subtle alarm tickled the back of his neck, and his fingers clutched the door handle without opening it.

He hadn't imagined footsteps. They were in a hurry now, moving away from his location. Punctuated by the slam of a vehicle door, he had to wonder if someone had been watching them. But a quick 360 didn't reveal any spies. Maybe his family's conversation about arson, and Corie's suspicion that someone had been inside her apartment while she'd been at school, were feeding his wary senses.

This wasn't a place where muggings and street crime

happened much anymore—and anyone with a lick of sense would think twice about coming after him. Matt could walk the walk when it came to holding his own in a physical confrontation. His firefighter training and lifting weights weren't the only skills he'd honed over the years.

Still, the tickle at his nape was never wrong when it came to fighting fires and the safety of the men and women on his Firehouse 13 team. Something wasn't right. But what he saw as intrusive might just be a curious neighbor, wondering what was going on over the old Taylor Butcher Shop, or why the loner of the Taylor clan, who'd never even brought a date to a family gathering, now had a kid in tow.

With no obvious threat in sight, Matt climbed in and locked the doors. After he started the engine, he cranked the heat and found Evan's curious green eyes watching him in the rearview mirror. "I'm going to let the truck warm up for a few minutes before we go."

Evan pushed up against his seat belt. "Can I use your watch to count how many minutes again?"

"Sure." Matt took his utility watch off his wrist and reached over the seat to show Evan the timer feature. "Now you set it for four minutes. When the alarm goes off, I'll hear it and we'll go."

"Sweet." Evan leaned back in his seat to play with the watch that fascinated him so. "We have twenty-four minutes before I have to be in bed," he announced. "After the truck warms up, we'll have twenty minutes to drive home."

Good math skills. He'd run through his multiplication problems in a matter of minutes, and gotten every answer right, before Matt gave him the okay to go in and play with Gideon Jr. "I'll get you home in eighteen."

"We'll have to run up the stairs if we only have two minutes."

"I'll race you." As soon as the watch beeped, Matt pulled out of his parking space. There was little traffic at this hour, and he quickly passed two blocks before stopping at the red light. Matt found Evan watching him in the mirror again. "Will there be someone at the diner to walk your mom to her car when she gets off work?"

"We don't have a car."

His guileless pronouncement rekindled Matt's suspicions. "Then how does she get to school and work and then come home?"

"The way we always do. We walk. Or when it's cold like this, we'll walk to the bus stop. It's not that far."

But it was late at night, she was a woman and she was alone. "Does she ever let you walk that far by yourself?"

"Un-uh."

"Then she shouldn't, either." Movement in the street behind him shifted his attention from Evan. A nondescript van pulled out of a parking space and drove up behind Matt's truck. The van wasn't speeding. But with its headlights blinding him in every mirror, he couldn't get a look at the driver, either. "Hey, bud. Why don't you set the timer for fifteen minutes. You time me to see if we get home before it beeps."

Matt was glad to see Evan concentrating on the watch, telling him the boy wasn't alarmed by the vehicle behind them. But he was an eight-year-old boy—he shouldn't have to be worried about strange coincidences and sixth senses warning him of danger. That was Matt's job. On impulse, he turned right before the light changed. When the van turned the corner behind him, Matt pulled his phone from his coat pocket and punched in a familiar number.

His brother Mark picked up on the second ring. "Did you miss me?"

"Do you mind stopping by my place on your way home?"

"No." Every bit of humor left Mark's tone. "What's up?"

Matt took another random corner, and the van followed. The warning at the nape of his neck couldn't be ignored. "I'm not sure. But I'd feel better if I had some backup."

Chapter Seven

"Hey, blondie."

"Come on, sugar—you know you miss us."

Great. Now the two men at the back of the bus were blowing kisses at her.

After that "courtesy" message her attorney's office in St. Louis had left on her phone tonight, she sure as hell didn't need this.

"As a courtesy, we are notifying all our clients that Owenson, Marsden & Heath may have had a breach in security subsequent to an electrical fire in our offices, in which several computers and most of our files were destroyed. While we are making every effort to ensure confidentiality while we sort through the remains of both paper and digital records, we are still in the process of accounting for all our data. Rest assured, backup systems were in place, and we are able to continue working on all of your current or upcoming needs. We are happy to report that Mr. Heath is at home now, recovering from injuries sustained in the fire. Our temporary offices will be housed at…"

She hadn't listened to the rest of the voice mail. Current and upcoming needs had nothing to do with her. Her only legal concerns were in the past. But a breach in security? Missing records? Her attorney injured in a fire?

To Corie, that meant only one thing. Kenny.

Was he responsible for that fire? Had he gotten access to her new identity and other personal records Mr. Heath had arranged for her? Had he burned the place down to cover up evidence that he had been in St. Louis? If he could track down her attorney, could he also find her here in Kansas City?

"Whatchya thinkin' about, sugar? Which one of us you'd like to get to know better first?"

Corie hugged her backpack tightly to her chest and stared at her hunkered reflection in the bus window and at the city lights that seemed to float past as she made her way home after closing the diner. Normally she found the ride home relaxing, and she enjoyed seeing parts of the city still decorated for Christmas or New Year's, especially when the lights reflected off the snow. But tonight, the world outside was a blur. Her pulse thundered in her ears, drowning out any fun or peaceful thoughts. And she was shivering, despite her coat and gloves and the bus's heater blowing across her feet.

She fought to keep Kenny's verbal abuse from playing in her head. *"What the hell's a study group? You're not going anywhere. You're good for only two things. If you weren't so damn frigid, it'd be three. You make me look good and you take care of my baby. Understand?"* The words might be different, but the tone was the same. Her reaction was, too.

This is not Kenny, Corie told herself, forcing herself to take deep, calming breaths. *There is no proof that he set that fire in St. Louis and found out about your new life. Your world isn't burning down around you.* The two men hassling her tonight weren't Kenny. Even at his worst, Kenny had been all about appearances—the right look, the right woman, associating with people of money and power. *Those two losers are just a couple of drunks who happened to get on your bus. You have value, Corie. You are strong. Think of the positives. Evan is safe. You are safe.*

She repeated the mantra again and again, just like her therapist had advised her. *Evan is safe. You are safe.*

Her feet throbbed with the length of her day at school and the long night at the diner. But tips had been good, she'd timed it just right so that she didn't have to wait outside in the cold for the bus to arrive and she'd had enough time on her last break to get on her laptop and track down the last source for the paper she was writing for her English language learners class. Except for that phone call and those two yahoos in the back, nights like this were all worth it, right?

She'd made the mistake of making eye contact with Jordan and Harve when they'd first stumbled onto the bus at the stop after hers. Apparently, a brief glance had been invitation enough for the two drunks to slide into the seats next to and across the aisle from her, introduce themselves and start hitting on her. At first, she'd thought they might try to rob her when Jordan had put his hands on the backpack in her lap and leaned into her. But then Harve had grabbed his crotch and run his tongue around his chapped lips, and she realized they weren't after money or her computer.

"Mr. Lee?" She'd wasted no time calling out to the fatherly Black man driving the bus. He'd ordered the two booze-scented men—one with scraggly red peach fuzz on his jaw that blended into the tattoos on his neck, and the other sporting a chest-length beard that had a broken pretzel stuck in it—to move, or he'd call the police and drop them off at the next stop.

With much vocal protest and a stumble onto a seat with a startled young man whose earbuds had tuned them out up to that intrusion, they'd made their way to the back of the bus, where they continued to be a nuisance to anyone with a pair of boobs between the ages of eighteen and fifty. And since Corie was currently the only passenger left who fit that description tonight, she was bearing the brunt of their lewd noises and whispered innuendoes.

"Just one drink, sugar?" That would be Harve, with the snack stuck in his facial hair. "We could have a nightcap at your place."

Once upon a time, when she was young and naive and believed every man could be a hero, she would have turned to Kenny to make them stop. And no doubt, with his resources and criminal connections, he would have. But that was before she realized he'd be protecting his property—not her feelings of fear or discomfort. Kenny would have made a threat or punched one of those rummies or tracked them down and torched their car to make the point that nobody embarrassed him by putting a move on the woman—or anything else—he considered his.

Tonight, she had to deal with this kind of crap on her own.

Or find an ally she could actually trust to have her best interests at heart.

Corie met the driver's gaze in his rearview mirror and silently pleaded for his help. "Knock it off!" he ordered, quieting the pair temporarily. "Sorry about that, Ms. Corie."

"Corie? Your name's Corie?"

"Corie what, sugar?"

The driver grumbled a curse and shook his head, realizing too late that he'd just given those two losers more information about her. Although she offered him a reassuring smile, she hoped Mr. Lee didn't repeat his threat about putting them off at the next stop because the next stop was hers. At least, here on the bus, she had the relative safety of the other passengers and driver to protect her—or at least bear witness to the harassment if anything should happen to her. Corie still had a cold walk back to her apartment once she stepped off this bus. She didn't relish being alone at night for the block and a half it would take her to get safely inside the locked foyer of her building if those men decided to follow her.

As the bus turned onto Wyandotte and drove up the hill toward her stop, Corie peeled off her gloves and stuffed them into her coat pockets. Potential frostbite would take a back seat to security tonight. Then she dug into her bag and pulled out her cell phone and pepper spray, squeezing one in each hand. She might not be able to outmuscle or outrun Jordan and Harve if they should decide to follow her and prolong this torture, but she could outthink them. She could plan ahead and give herself options for escape. Then she shrugged her backpack onto her shoulders and prepared to book it as fast as she could to her building. If there was one thing she'd learned from her years with Kenny, it was to be prepared for any- and everything.

And to do whatever was necessary to keep herself and Evan safe.

Moving quickly, she slid out of her seat and hurried down the aisle to sit in the very first seat beside the stairs. She intended to be down the steps and out the door just as soon as it opened.

"Whoa. Slow down, sugar. We'll walk you home." Jordan lurched to his feet, with Harve shuffling after him.

"Sit down," Carl Lee ordered when he saw them coming down the aisle behind her. "This isn't your stop." He glanced across the aisle and whispered to Corie, "You hustle on out of here the moment I stop. I'll try to keep them inside."

Harve snickered and plopped down in the spot behind Corie, dangling his arm over the top of her seat. "Maybe we need some fresh air, old man." She jerked away when his fingers brushed against her ponytail. "Besides, we wouldn't want our little woman walking home by herself so late now, would we?"

Corie practically threw herself against the partition in front of her seat and whirled around to tell the creep to back off. "I am *not* your little woman, and I *don't* need you to walk me home."

Mistake! She'd engaged them. Now they saw her response as a personal invitation to increase their taunts. "Ooh, she's feistier than I thought she was going to be." Jordan grinned from ear to ear.

"I like 'em feisty." Harve rose to his feet, and his long beard fell over the top of her seat. How she'd dearly love to yank it as hard as she could. Maybe he'd bite his tongue when his chin hit the seat, and that would shut him up.

Both men laughed. Mr. Lee muttered something under his breath and pulled his radio from the dash. Was he going to report these two? Call the police?

She turned her back to the men as the brakes hissed and the bus began to slow. She tapped 9-1-1 into her own phone and prepared to push the call button if she had to.

Then she peered through the glass and saw the tall man standing beneath the shell of the bus stop. Silhouetted against the fluorescent lights, his height and bulk were emphasized by the insulated winter coat he wore. Like a beacon in the midst of a stormy sea, Matt Taylor's broad shoulders and immovable presence showed her the way to the safe harbor she needed.

Relief, gratitude beyond measure and maybe even anticipation surged through her veins and she shot to her feet. Bless his big, bad self for showing up and being the friend she needed right now.

"Matt!" Corie was down the stairs and out the door the moment it opened.

Without any hesitation or warning, she launched herself at him. She shoved her phone and pepper spray into her pockets and grabbed the collar of his coat with both fists, pulling him toward her as she stretched up on tiptoe and pushed her lips against his. His startled breath didn't surprise her—she hadn't given him much of a heads-up. But she didn't expect his firm mouth to slide over hers in answer to her desperate ploy. She didn't expect the rasp of his late-night beard stubble to tease her skin with its own subtle caress. She didn't expect the frisson of heat that tingled across her lips and shocked much-needed warmth into her blood when his mouth settled over hers in a brief, potent kiss.

The kiss was longer than she intended, shorter than she wanted, and left the ground shaking beneath her feet as she dropped to her heels. Matt's lips chased after hers as gravity broke the contact between them. And Corie was far too tempted to palm the back of the black stocking cap he wore and guide his mouth right back to where she wanted it.

But the bus driver's warning to the men behind her reminded her that throwing herself at Matt was a survival tactic, not a mutual routine she had any right to pursue. She swallowed her shock and forced herself to continue the charade, although she could only manage a breathless whisper. "Hi, sweetheart."

"Sweetheart?" He rubbed his hands up and down her arms and his face hovered above hers, frowning in confusion until he heard Harve and Jordan's harassment.

"Hey, sugar, wait for us." The bearded man scrambled to the stairs behind her. "Don't you close these doors, old man."

"You said we'd have smooth sailin' with her, Harve. If I have to mess with that guy, then I want extra—"

"Shut up, Jordy."

Corie didn't need to explain her overly friendly greeting.

Matt's expression was cold, fierce and eerily silent as he lifted his gaze and looked over the top of her head to meet Jordan and Harve. He pried Corie's hands from the front of his coat and moved around her. Straightening to his towering height, he didn't have to say a word to stop the two men in their tracks.

Jordan toppled onto the curb in his haste to back away from the imposing welcome. Harve grabbed the sleeve of Jordan's coat and tugged him to his feet and up the stairs. "Get on back here, Jordy. This isn't our stop, after all." His dark eyes rounded like shiny black beetles as he nodded to Corie. "We'll be seeing you, Ms. Corie."

Jordan puckered his lips. "Bye-bye, sugar."

Just as Corie flinched back half a step at that final unwanted gesture, Matt strode forward. He boarded the bus, each step a purposeful stride. He stopped beside the driver and watched Harve and Jordan beat a hasty retreat down the aisle, all the way to their seats at the back. Then Matt lifted his coat to pull out his billfold and hand a business card to Mr. Lee. "You see those two hassling Corie again, you call me."

"Kansas City's Bravest." Carl took the card and nodded his ready agreement. "Yes, sir. You all be safe now."

"Good night, Mr. Lee," Corie called up to him as Matt rejoined her. "Thank you."

"Good night, Ms. Corie. Mr. Taylor." The Black man nodded and closed the door. With the hum of the motor grinding into gear, the bus pulled away.

A chill from the damp, wintry air seeped through the wool of her coat and Corie hugged her arms around her waist. But the cold temperature wasn't the only thing that made her shiver. Harve and Jordan pressed their faces to the back windows, their eyes only leaving her when the two high-fived each other over the top of the seat.

She startled at Matt's touch and the sudden infusion of heat as he draped his arm around her shoulders and tucked her to his side. Playing his part of half a couple even better than she was playing hers, he was also watching the two men until the lights from the bus stop and streetlamp could no longer pierce the windows and her tormenters were swallowed up into the shadows.

Corie stood there, leaning into Matt's warmth long enough for her to realize that she hadn't put her gloves back on. Though stiff with cold, her fingers were fisted into the padded nylon of his black insulated jacket, clinging to him as though she had every right to attach herself to him for comfort or use him as a human heating pad. Shaking off those survival instincts that seemed to have her continually reaching for him, Corie released her grip and stepped away. She dug her gloves out of her pockets and slipped them back on. "I'm sorry about that kiss. I just…" She glanced down the street where the bus had merged into late-night traffic, then tilted her face to Matt's. "I needed them to stop. I suspected if they thought I was *with* you… It worked. Thank you."

He didn't seem to hear her apology. Or care that she'd taken advantage of his willingness to help her.

He didn't have anyone with him, either.

Where was Evan? Kenny had found them!

Corie tamped down the flare of panic that grabbed hold whenever she didn't know Evan's exact location. *Too soon to worry. Too soon.*

"Do you know those two?" Matt asked.

She shook her head, looking around. No, she hadn't seen them before tonight. Oh, damn. The panic was winning. They were all alone at this bus stop. There was no child here with them. Her apartment was a block and a half away. Was Evan at home all by himself again? She didn't see Matt's truck. There was a small group of patrons outside the bar down the street, huddling up to smoke their cigarettes—but no one anywhere close to Evan's age. Where was her son? She'd trusted Matt with one job. Okay, maybe two now that Jordan and Harve had inserted themselves into her life tonight—but she'd trusted Matt with the one thing more important than anything else in the world—her son.

"They seemed to know you," Matt went on matter-of-factly. "Why would they think you'd be an easy mark for them? 'Smooth sailing'?"

Corie even made the ridiculous move of peeking behind Matt's broad back, looking for her freckle-faced angel. "Where's Evan?"

Matt turned so they were facing each other again. His deep, patiently modulated voice barely changed its timbre, even though he hunched his shoulders a fraction to bring his gaze closer to hers and demand she focus on what he was saying. "Sound asleep on my sofa. My brother and his fiancée are with him. Ev is fine. Tell me about those two men."

Matt's eyes captured her attention. Unlike Harve's cold, creepy beetle eyes, their warm brown intensity moved through her like the potent drink they resembled. His coffee-colored eyes calmed her panic and chased away the chill of remembered fears. Evan was safe. Matt was a stand-up, trustworthy man who wouldn't do anything to endanger her son. *He's not Kenny.*

And as rational thought returned, the point Matt was making registered. Was it her imagination, or had Harve sounded remarkably articulate for a drunk who'd been slurring every word a few minutes earlier? "He's asleep at your place? Evan's okay?"

"Yes. Are you?" Matt slowly straightened, his gaze never wavering from hers. His gloved hands fisted down at his sides, relaxed, then fisted again, as though he wanted to reach for her, but was holding himself back from making contact.

She wouldn't have minded. After the past six years of avoiding men—at first because she'd assumed they were all like Kenny and his thuggish cohorts, and later because work, school and being a hypervigilant single mom didn't allow time for relationships—she wouldn't have minded if Matt Taylor reached for her, at all.

Corie's lips relaxed into a wry smile and she nodded. "I'm fine. Thanks to you." Whether Matt was being exceedingly patient or endearingly shy, Corie wanted that connection he was too polite to initiate. She'd once been a confident young woman who'd gone after what her mother had told her she wanted—what she naively thought she'd wanted, too—until a kidnapping and death threats and Kenny's violent, obsessive world had scared that brave young woman into submission. It was nice to feel a little of her confidence returning with this man. She slipped her arm through Matt's and stepped toward the curb. "Could we head home now?"

"As long as you talk to me." He rested a leather-gloved hand over hers where she clung to his forearm, revealing that he liked sharing that friendly link with her, too, and didn't want her pulling away. The man was warm, and he made her feel safe. And his kiss had awakened something dormant and too-long ignored inside her. She wasn't going anywhere.

Falling into step beside him, Corie shared the bare bones of her bus ride home. "They got on at the stop just after the diner. You know—too much to drink and not enough action at whatever bar they'd come out of. I tried to keep my head down, but they spotted me, decided I was their chosen target. Mr. Lee told them to move—and they did. But that didn't shut them up. Then they became a nuisance to everyone on the bus. Only now I wonder if it was all an act. Harve seemed to sober up pretty quickly once you showed up."

"I have that effect on people."

Whether he meant to be funny or not, Corie smiled and pressed her cheek against his shoulder. The material of his jacket was cold against her skin, but she savored the supple hardness and promised warmth of the muscle she felt underneath. They crossed the street and walked a whole block like that, with Corie hugging herself around Matt's arm and his hand covering hers. Matt's bulk blocked the worst of the wind, and his ever-watchful eyes that scanned their surroundings and occasionally settled on her made her feel protected. Simply walking down the street arm in arm with Matt felt normal. Intimate. And far more romantic than any grand gesture Kenny had ever used to try to charm her. "It's just weird. Weird things are happening around me lately," she admitted. "First the fires, and I think someone's been in my apartment. That stupid phone call. Now those two idiots giving me grief."

"What phone call?"

Corie's breath clouded on a puff of frustration. Had she actually said that out loud? She tried to explain in a way that didn't make her sound like the completely paranoid woman she was. "A voice mail from my attorney's assistant in St. Louis. There was a fire in their office."

"Was anyone hurt?"

"My attorney sustained minor injuries, but he's doing fine now. I guess they lost several documents in the fire."

"Were any of the destroyed documents yours?"

She shrugged. She had immediately imagined the worst, but she truly didn't know. "It was just an FYI call."

Matt's fingers tightened briefly on hers before he slid his hands into the pockets of his coat. She might have imagined him hugging his elbows to his torso, keeping their arms linked together, encouraging her to remain at his side. But as he glanced over her head to track the line of cars and trucks coming through the intersection behind them as the lights changed, she sensed something about his posture had changed, grown wary. He wanted his hands free to…to what? "You didn't see a white van following the bus, did you?"

"No. It's hard to see much besides the lights through the windows at night." She studied the vehicles that rolled past them. Not a van of any kind in sight. The thrill she'd just admitted to herself at having Matt meet her at the bus stop to walk her home vanished. Had he seen something she had missed? "Why?"

"I saw an unfamiliar vehicle in the neighborhood earlier. It followed us from Grandma's place."

"Followed?" Corie stopped, yanking her arm from his. Futile thrills and chivalry and logical explanations be damned. There *was* something wrong. "Why didn't you say something?"

Matt turned. He cupped her elbows and ran his hands up and down her arms. "My brothers who are cops are looking into it. The van didn't come to our building or parking garage. I lost it by taking the scenic route home."

She didn't want reassurances. She wanted facts. She knew better than to dismiss the suspicion in his words and posture. "The van was following you? You're certain? Did you see the driver? Is Evan okay? Was he scared?" The last time she'd felt like the world was falling apart around her, it had been. She didn't intend to dismiss the things that struck her as odd and be caught off guard and forced into doing something she regretted again. "I need to see Evan. Right now."

This time, Matt draped his arm around her shoulders and tucked her to his side. His stride seemed to be longer now, forcing her to hurry her pace. "As far as I could tell, he spent the whole time playing with my watch on the drive home. I doubt he noticed the van."

Corie shook her head, feeling equally doubtful. "He notices everything."

"He does. I crashed through a wall tonight, made a lot of noise. He came running to make sure I was okay." She paused and glanced up at him. "I was," he answered her unspoken question, pulling her back into a quick step beside him. "Evan is, too. My brother Mark is with him. My brothers Pike and Alex are working on tracking down the van, although I only got a partial plate. Chances are the guy was scoping out my truck to see if he could steal it. I was more worried about you being out here by yourself."

"I'm fine. I'm going to be fine," she amended. "I've handled worse than a couple of drunks on the bus. Evan is my only concern."

Matt's arm tightened around her, partially lifting her to keep pace with his stride as they climbed the granite steps to their building. He swiped his key card and led her inside. Even being in the lobby, cut off from the cold, windy night, she felt chilled. Seven years ago, when the trouble began with Kenny—the worst year of her life—the terror had all started with someone following her and her son.

Matt punched the elevator call button. "You won't do him any good if something happens to you."

Corie hurried inside and pressed the button for the seventh floor. "I'm a grown-up. I can take care of myself. He just turned eight. He's trusting and curious and all I have that's worth anything." She was clearly rattled by the incident or she wouldn't still be clinging to Matt. Once she realized her fingers were clutched in the side of his coat, she tried to release him. But her grip seemed to be locked in place, and, damn it, her eyes were stinging with tears.

"Hey." As the elevator doors closed, Matt framed her jaw between his big hands, tilting her face up to his. "Next time you work late, let me know. I will pick you up. And if I'm on shift, I'll send one of my brothers or my dad."

She shook her head between his hands. "We've been riding the bus for months. We're not your responsibility. I can't ask you to—"

"You're not coming home on your own after dark again." He emphasized his resolute pronouncement by tightening his fingers against her hair and the sides of her neck, gently preventing another shake of her head. A soft huff that could be a wry laugh stirred the bangs on her forehead. "It's bad for my blood pressure."

"*Your* blood pressure?" She reached up to wind her fingers around his wrists. "*I'm* the one who's freaking out."

He stroked his thumb across her cheek. His leather glove was cool against her skin, but his firm touch and deep voice swept aside the world long enough for her to take a deep breath. "Let me do this small thing. Please."

She needed to think, not react. She needed to use her brain, not her emotions. And most importantly, she needed to get her mental stuff together so she wouldn't frighten Evan. Matt's patience and no-nonsense caring gave her enough of a break from her maternal panic to dial it back a notch. She believed him when he said Evan was safe. For that, she was grateful. But she didn't intend to become a burden to him. Besides, if these odd events did have anything to do with Kenny Norwell, anyone who got involved with her would be in danger. "We're already an imposition. It shouldn't be your problem."

He didn't try to lie and say she and the recent events surrounding her and Evan weren't an upheaval in his life. He didn't tell her not to worry. He didn't wheel and deal and promise to take care of her problems for her in exchange for her silence or a roll in the hay or custody of her son the way Kenny would have.

Instead, Matt planted himself in front of her like the unbending oak he was and held out his hand. "Give me your phone." He tugged his gloves off with his teeth and held them there while he typed his number into her phone and handed it back to her. "This is faster than pulling my card out of your bag." The boyish move and garbled sentence were as endearing as that unexpected response to her kiss had been intoxicating. She plucked his gloves from between his lips and held them for him while he pulled out his cell and typed in her number. Now that he could talk clearly, he added, "If you prefer the bus, one of us will ride with you. Offering you a lift doesn't mean you owe me anything. Just promise you'll call."

When he was done, she tucked each glove into the appropriate pocket of his jacket, just as she did with Evan almost every day when they got home from school. But instead of sending him on to his room to play, as she would a child, Corie wound her arms around Matt's waist and hugged him tightly, taking note of every hard plane and solid muscle pressed against her. Even though she was of average height, she scarcely reached his shoulders. Still, it felt like a perfect fit when his arms folded around her and he lowered his head to rest his chin against the crown of her hair. Corie nestled in, oddly sad that the elevator was slowing to a stop. "You're a better friend than I deserve, Matt. But you may not want to get involved with me."

"Maybe I do. Maybe I already am." The elevator doors opened, and he released her to walk side by side down the hallway together. "Have a little faith in me, okay?"

Corie reached for his hand and laced their fingers together. "Trusting you is the easy part."

Chapter Eight

Corie pushed open the door the moment Matt unlocked it, anxious to see Evan after hearing Matt's suspicion about the white van.

As he ushered her inside the shadowed living room, they were greeted by a slightly shorter, equally broad version of Matt. Although his eyes were blue to Matt's warm brown color, there was no mistaking that this was his brother. Mark Taylor pressed a finger against his lips, urging them to whisper as he nodded toward the couch where Evan was fast asleep with his arm thrown around his dragon and Matt's watch strapped to his wrist. A statuesque redhead in a paint-stained sweatshirt entered from the kitchen, drying her hands on a towel. She smiled a greeting to Corie and Matt without saying a word.

"My brother Mark," Matt whispered behind her. "His fiancée, Amy Hall. This is Corie, Evan's mom."

Although her eyes barely left her sleeping child, and the relief flooding through her made it difficult to speak, Corie managed to thank the couple before hurrying across the room. She peeled off her gloves and knelt beside the couch to peer into Evan's sweetly in-nocent face as he snored softly atop a throw pillow. She brushed a lock of shaggy brown hair off his freckled cheek and cupped the back of his head. He was perfectly fine—exhausted from what had no doubt been an ex-citing evening for him, but fine. Kenny hadn't found them. Kenny hadn't taken her son from her again. Ex-haling a sigh of relief that echoed through the room, she pushed to her feet, adjusted the afghan covering him and kissed his cheek.

"Better?" Matt asked. He must have followed right behind her.

She looked up at him and nodded. "You were right. He's okay. It's just…a mother has to know." She turned Matt's watch on Evan's slender wrist to unbuckle it. "You'd better take this now or you may never see it again."

Matt stopped her fingers and slipped it back down Evan's slender wrist. "Let him keep it for tonight. I think it makes him feel safe, like he can cope with any-thing that stresses him."

She wasn't sure it was the watch so much as whom the watch represented. There were a lot of things about this man that made a person feel safe. Corie squeezed her hand around Matt's forearm, thanking him for the consideration. "I'll make sure we return it in the morn-ing."

Corie felt a tug from the opposite side as Amy linked arms with her and pulled her toward the bright lights of the kitchen. "Come with me. Let's go where we don't have to whisper. I made some hot chocolate to warm us all up. And I want to show you the drawing Evan made." Her voice grew louder and more exuberant as they left Evan snoozing in the living room. "I'm going to turn it into one of my garden aliens, a miniature one he can keep in his room. If that's okay. He said he had a spot for it."

Amy handed Corie the colored pencil drawing sitting on the table and hurried to the stove to fill a couple of mugs with hot chocolate. "Garden aliens?"

"Unbutton your coat and sit for a few minutes." Clearly, Amy felt at home here in Matt's apartment, as she gestured to a chair at the rustic wood farm table. With Matt's penchant for working with his hands, she wondered if he had restored, or even built it himself. She didn't get time to ask as Amy pointed out the whorls of purple, red and yellow on Evan's drawing. "I see dragon overtones, which will be fun to incorporate. Evan is certainly bold with his color choices. I find that inspiring."

Should she be worried about the ever-expanding army of dragons guarding Evan's room?

Mark strolled into the kitchen, picking up a half-empty mug from the table and carrying it to his fiancée for seconds as she tore open pouches of instant cocoa and poured hot water from the kettle into each mug. "Amy's an artist. She works mostly in metals. She's set up shop in my garage."

"Only because mine burned down this past summer." She handed Corie and Matt each a steaming mug of cocoa before sitting in the chair next to Corie's. She thrust out her left hand. "Here's an example of my handiwork. My engagement ring."

Corie was left with little choice but to examine the twisted filigree work around the diamond solitaire. It was certainly one of a kind…as she suspected Amy was, too. "What a unique, beautiful ring."

Mark squeezed his hands around Amy's shoulders, and she leaned back into him, holding her hand up to admire the jewelry. "Mark gave me the diamond on a plain white-gold band when he proposed, with his blessing to turn it into whatever I wanted. I melted it down and created the two hearts knotted together around the diamond. The wedding bands I'm making will be plainer because of Mark's work."

Corie cradled the steaming mug in her hands and shrugged. "Wow. You're making your own wedding jewelry, and I don't even have a hobby."

Matt stood at the counter next to the stove, stirring his hot chocolate. "Because you're working or studying all the time. Or doing stuff with Evan. Not everybody could handle all that on their plate as well as you do."

She smiled at him across the room, silently thanking him for the shout-out of praise. And, if she wasn't mistaken, that slight tilt at the corner of his firm mouth meant he was smiling back.

Finally feeling herself warming up, Corie shed her coat while Matt and Mark joined them at the table. She'd had every intention of walking Evan across the hall and getting out of Matt's hair so that they wouldn't be any more of an imposition on their evening. But the Taylor brothers and Amy were making her feel like a welcome guest. No, they were making her feel like a friend. Corie couldn't recall the last time she'd sat down with people her own age and talked about things not related to teaching, classes, work or legal matters. They chatted for another thirty minutes or so while they sipped their cocoa. She got the gist of the wedding Mark and Amy were planning for the summer on the grounds of her grandmother's farm. She heard a couple of stories about the Lucky 13 crew at the firehouse where the brothers both worked. Matt didn't add much more than a shrug to Mark's assertion that Matt had pulled him not once, but twice, from a fire. Even though Mark and Amy dominated the conversation, there was no mistaking the way they included both her and Matt with teasing gibes, complimentary observations about Evan and interesting questions that helped them get to know Corie while she got to know them.

She imagined the conversation would have gone on a good deal longer until the moment she failed to mask a yawn. She quickly pressed her hand over her mouth. "Sorry about that. It's not the company, I promise."

Mark pushed his chair away from the table as Amy squeezed Corie's hand and offered her a rueful smile. "My bad. I ramble whenever I start talking about marrying this guy. Matt's learned to put up with me." She glanced across the table and winked at the man beside Corie. "I think he might even like me."

"He does," Matt replied. "I said I'd be in the wedding, didn't I?"

Amy rose from the table and circled around to hug Matt from behind. "You did."

"Come on, Red." Mark tugged on Amy's hand. "Let's let these guys get some sleep. Corie put in a long day, and I've got a long one tomorrow." Matt pulled out Corie's chair in a sweetly old-fashioned gesture, and they all went into the living room, automatically dropping their voices as they got closer to Evan. After helping Amy into her coat, Mark shook hands with Matt and the two men bumped shoulders in a manly hug. "See you at work, bro."

"Thanks for helping out tonight."

"Like you haven't done the same for me."

Amy hugged Matt and then reached for Corie, her hug turning into a secretive whisper. "Matt's a good guy. The best there is. A bit of an odd duck—"

"Red?" Mark chided, pulling his fiancée away from Corie. "What did we say about matchmaking?"

Amy's conspiratorial whisper included Mark now. "That he's slow as molasses and might need a little nudge?"

"And on that note, we'll be going." Mark opened the door and ushered his fiancée into the hallway ahead of him. "Nice to meet you, Corie." But apparently, he wasn't immune to the matchmaking bug, either. He looked beyond her to Matt and winked. "Good night, Molasses."

Matt palmed his brother's face and shoved him out the door. Mark laughed, reached for Amy's hand, and the engaged couple headed for the elevator as Matt closed the door behind them. When he faced her, she thought she detected the faintest tinge of a blush peeking through his shadow of beard stubble. "Sorry about that. Those two can be…aggressively friendly."

Corie turned to hide the blush she was certain was

staining her own cheeks and hurried back to the kitchen, where she carried the mugs to the sink and rinsed them out. "It's obvious they love you very much. It must be nice to have family you can depend on, even on short notice like this."

Moving with surprising stealth for a man his size, Matt appeared at the counter beside her and opened the dishwasher to place the mugs she handed him inside. "You don't have family? I suspected not here in Kansas City because you and Ev are always alone. You never have any company. But no family anywhere? You mentioned St. Louis earlier."

"That's where I grew up. Only child. I have a mother and a stepdad. He was pretty decent. But Mom and I severed ties. I miss the idea of having a mom and a grandmother for Evan, but I don't miss her." She could read the unspoken *why?* in his eyes. Corie shrugged and wet the dishcloth to wipe down the stove and countertop. It wasn't hard to talk about anymore. She'd made her peace with her choices when she'd changed her name and left St. Louis. "I told you my ex hurt a lot of people. But he also had a lot of money. Most of it made illegally, I discovered, doing jobs for other criminals. But Mom was willing to overlook that little detail as long as he showered her with gifts and kept me in a beautiful house that was way too big for the three of us."

"*Kept* you?"

Corie met a wall of Matt Taylor demanding answers and returned to the sink without meeting his probing gaze. He seemed to intuit that the irony of her word choices was more literal that most people might suspect. "He kidnapped Evan when I separated from him. The police didn't call it kidnapping since he was still a custodial parent. But if I wanted to be with my son, I had to be with Kenny."

"You could have divorced him, sued for full custody."

Corie shook her head. She'd been a young, vulnerable mess, isolated from any support system and afraid for her life. "The woman I was back then couldn't have."

"But you got stronger. Norwell's no longer in your life. You do have full custody, right?"

Corie nodded. "I legally changed our names and moved away from that nightmare. Started life over on my terms."

"Is that why the call from your attorney's office upset you? Do you think your mother or your ex was trying to locate who and where you are now?"

"My attorney does have that information. But Heath's office isn't even sure if anything is missing. They were calling all of his clients to tell us about the break-in, just to cover themselves legally, I suppose." She'd been so careful for so long, as had her attorney. As far as the world knew, Katie Norwell and her son, Danny, had disappeared from the face of the earth. "Kenny stayed in Jefferson City after he was released from prison. And my mother wouldn't know the first thing about break-ins and fires."

Matt started the dishwasher, perhaps giving her a few moments to tamp down her emotions. "It takes an unusually strong character to start over without any family or friends to help you."

His compliment warmed her. "When Kenny got arrested for arson and eventually sent to prison, I thought my mother would finally see him for the monster he was, we'd mend old wounds and become a family again." By the time she'd hung up the dishcloth and dried her hands, she'd found the composure to tilt her eyes to Matt's. "My mother encouraged me to marry Kenny in the first place—and she criticized me for divorcing him and taking his son from him, said that was a mistake I couldn't come back from. After all, arson is a victimless crime, she said."

If Matt was a more effusive man, he would have scoffed right then. "Tell that to the people who've lost everything they own. Who've lost the security of a roof over their heads—or worse, a pet or family member. Whether anyone dies or not, there are victims."

A fist of some long-buried grief over all she'd lost squeezed around her heart. Some parts of her past *were* hard to talk about, after all. Leaving the kitchen, Corie went to her sleeping son, sprawled on the couch, looking innocent and secure in a way she could never be. She reached down to feather her fingers through his hair and smooth the wispy spikes off his forehead. "You'd think a parent would do anything to protect their child. I would. I have. My mother's last words to me were, 'Go to him and beg his forgiveness.'" Corie shivered as though the air-conditioning had kicked on and pulled the front of her cardigan tightly around her polyester uniform. "He hurt people for a living. He put me in the hospital and kidnapped Evan so I'd go back to him. It took Kenny going to prison for us to get away from him—and she wanted me to beg his forgiveness?"

Without any warning, Matt pulled her into his arms and hugged her. Even with her crossed arms wedged between them, she felt his heat and unyielding strength. For several endless moments, she collapsed a little into the shielding bliss of his embrace. Just as she'd caressed Evan's hair a minute earlier, Matt tunneled his fingers into the hair beneath her ponytail, lifting its weight from her scalp and massaging the tension there. She didn't need any words—she could feel his empathy. But he offered her words, anyway. "Not everyone makes a good parent. My birth parents were drunk or high a lot. Mark and I barely had any supervision. I was literally playing with fire the night our house burned down, and they died. They were passed out in the living room. I managed to get Mark out. But I couldn't get them to wake up. If they'd been better parents…"

"Oh, Matt." She pulled her arms free to wind them around his waist and hugged him tight. "How old were you?"

"It doesn't matter."

"How old?" she insisted, tugging on a fistful of the flannel shirt he wore. "You said you were younger than Evan when you…acted out."

"Four."

"Only four?" She found the strong beat of his heart beneath her ear and nestled her cheek there. Her own heart was crying for the child he'd once been. "How frightened you must have been."

"I'm not trying to compare my pain to yours—or

make any less of it. I just want you to know that I understand what it means to not have someone be there when you need them."

Corie rubbed her nose into the soft nap of Matt's flannel shirt, inhaling his honest, hardworking masculine scent. Kenny had never simply held her. He'd wanted her on his arm to show her off to his friends and employers, or in his bed for what she'd naively thought was unsatisfying sex simply because she was inexperienced. She'd eventually learned that the sex had never been about her at all, certainly not after she'd given him the baby boy he'd wanted. Holding Matt, being held by him, was a new experience, an incredibly addictive one that she didn't seem to have any willpower to move away from. Standing in Matt's arms, his body flush and warm and strong against hers, was like a soothing tonic and a sensual awakening all rolled into one.

"I only wanted them to notice me," Matt went on, his fingers hypnotically stroking the back of her neck above her collar. "Mark was the baby. He was cute. I was the…extra. Even at four, I knew we weren't a normal, *Leave It to Beaver* family." Her arms tightened as she imagined him as a lonely, neglected little boy. "I wanted them to feel something—fear, panic, maybe a little worry about Mark and me. *I* wanted to feel something."

"Like you were safe. Like someone cared enough to stop you from doing something dangerous. You probably blamed yourself for their deaths. They were the adults. They should have taken care of you."

Some of her hair caught in the stubble of his beard

as he nodded. "I thank God every day that the Taylors adopted Mark and me. Alex and Pike, too. We were all in the same foster home. Not everyone is lucky enough to have a family like ours."

Matt's lips grazed her hair and Corie wanted to sink into him—hold him like this through the entire night. There was a joke in there somewhere about them both being the offspring of selfish, clueless parents. But a betrayal like that might still be too painful for him to joke about. Wanting to ease his pain—or find solace for her own—wasn't what their relationship was about.

Or was it? Had fate led her to the apartment across the hall from Matt because he was the rare man who understood what she'd been through? Was she drawn to him because she felt the pull of pain and secrets that resembled her own? Was his reserved, quiet intensity meant to resurrect the confident, outgoing woman she'd once been?

Despite these few minutes of happiness and normalcy and an unexpected desire to take this embrace to the next level, another yawn reminded her of the reality of her life. A wry chuckle shook through her, and she loosened her grip on the back of Matt's shirt. Feelings for Matt were just a foolish wish at this late hour. "Again, it's not the company." She was a little disappointed at how easily Matt let her pull away. But the man was nothing if not imminently practical. She should be glad that at least one of them could show a little sense. "It's late. I'd better get Evan into his own bed or I'll never get him up for school in the morning."

"I'll carry him."

Corie retrieved her coat and gathered up Evan's belongings while Matt picked up the sleeping boy and carried him to his bed across the hall. Something primal and utterly female stirred in Corie's womb at the strong paternal image of Matt gently placing her son in his bed. He took equal care setting Evan's protective dragon on the headboard shelf and hanging Evan's coat on the back of his chair while she tucked him in. After turning on the night-light, she followed Matt to the front door.

The hot firefighter next door would make a wonderful father. She had a feeling Matt would be good at a lot of things, because he was patient and observant and supportive and caring. Protecting others seemed to be hard-wired into his DNA, and that chest, those arms, that butt in a pair of jeans and…oh, hell. She might come with some extra responsibility and emotional baggage, but she was a healthy, needy, grown woman whose hormones had gotten a hold of her.

Matt turned in the hallway. "I'll wait until you lock the dead—"

"Thank you for everything tonight." Corie might just be making the biggest mistake of her new life when she braced one hand against his chest, slid the other behind his neck and stretched up on tiptoe to capture his mouth in a kiss. She darted her tongue out to taste the firm line of his bottom lip, then felt it soften when she tugged it between her lips.

And then she realized he wasn't touching her. Her fingers were clutching the straight line of short, ticklish hair at the back of his head and his hands were fisted at his sides. Although she'd elicited a brief response when she'd suckled his lower lip, he wasn't kissing her. And she didn't think that husky huff from his chest was a groan of ecstasy.

Corie quickly released him and retreated half a step as the heat of embarrassment crept up her neck. "I'm sorry."

His fingers pulsed against his palms. "I said you didn't have to do anything you're not comfortable with. Just because my brother and Amy can't keep their hands to themselves doesn't mean I expect you to—"

"No, you said I needed to *tell* you when I wasn't comfortable with something." Her embarrassment gave way to a burst of anger, then settled into confusion. "It's a thank-you kiss, Matt. I didn't suck up my courage and *pretend* to kiss you. I wanted to do that." Nope. Here came the embarrassment again. "Unless you aren't okay with that? I mean, I know I'm out of practice, but when I kissed you at the bus stop, you sort of kissed me back. And the way you held me in your apartment, I thought…" She raked all ten fingers through hair, pulling out most of her ponytail. "Was I taking advantage—?"

"No. You can kiss me or touch me any time, any way you like." He almost sounded angry as he dipped his head toward hers and ground the words through his teeth. He snapped up straight, as though the vehemence of his response surprised him. He glanced away for a moment, gathering his thoughts before he looked back to her. "That didn't come out right." His hand batted the air and she could see him warring with whatever words he was having trouble expressing. He batted the air again, and then he feathered his fingers into the hair she'd pulled loose and the internal debate seemed to resolve itself when she didn't pull away from his touch. He smoothed the hair behind her ear and settled his hand against the side of her neck, easing her own uncertainty. "I would like to kiss you again sometime." His tone had quieted to that sexy, deliberate timbre that told her he was saying exactly what he was thinking. "For real. Not for show. Not for any reason other than… I want to kiss you."

Well, as declarations of desire went, that was hot. And it was really good for her ego to know they were on the same wavelength, after all. She smiled and reached up to touch his handsome mouth. "I'll keep that in mind." He just wanted her to know that she could move this budding relationship along at whatever pace she needed to—but that he was interested in pursuing it. She hoped he understood that she was interested, too, and that he didn't need to be shy about voicing his feelings with her. Maybe he'd also learn that giving in to his impulses didn't mean he'd frighten her the way Kenny had. Corie drew her hand down his chest before pulling back to the door. "Good night, Matt."

He touched the corner of her mouth and traced her smile with the tip of his finger, sparking an electric current that curled through her all the way down to her toes. "Good night."

When he nodded and pulled away without a kiss, she tried not to be disappointed. As she closed the door and leaned back against it, she reminded herself that she wasn't the only one who might be cautious about putting themselves out there. Matt had held her and touched her and listened and shared and awakened her heart. She closed her eyes and smiled. Good grief, she was falling hard for that one. She was feeling hopeful that she could have a normal life one day. Maybe she could even have that loving husband and big family she'd always dreamed about.

"Mom?" She opened her eyes to the shadowy darkness to find Evan stumbling into the living room.

"Hey, little man." Corie hurried to meet him and gently turn him back toward his bedroom. "What are you doing up?"

"I wanted to make sure you were home, and you were okay."

Corie nearly stumbled over the threshold as her heart seized up with his concern for her. Maybe *normal* was never really going to be an option for them. Not as long as Kenny Norwell had this influence over their lives.

"Yes, sweetie, I'm okay. Matt said you are, too." Now that he was partially awake, she helped him pull off his jeans and slip into his pajamas. "Come on. Let's get you back to bed."

He reached up to touch his dragon before climbing into bed again. "I really like Matt, Mom."

She pulled up the covers. "I like him, too."

"His grandma bakes cookies, and I made a new friend. Gideon doesn't go to my school, but we built a castle together. Can he come over and play sometime?" The big yawns she'd had over at Matt's were contagious. Evan seemed determined to get all his words out before he drifted off to sleep again. "Mark's funny. He calls Amy Red because of her red hair, and Pike calls Alex Shrimp because he's short..." Another yawn indicated this conversation wouldn't last long. "Oh, and Matt won the ax-chopping contest."

"The what?" Alarm flared but quickly went away because Evan was out, no doubt finally relaxing and dreaming happy thoughts judging by the smile on his face. Corie leaned over to give him another kiss. "Good night, little man. I love you."

She turned out the bedside lamp and left the door slightly ajar. It sounded like he'd had a grand adventure with Matt and his family tonight. There was definitely a little idolizing going on there. But she couldn't blame him. She seemed to have a thing for the firefighter next door, too.

As she headed down the hallway to her own bedroom, she heard one of the neighborhood cats who prowled the fire escapes looking for handouts or a warm spot to curl up scratching at her window. At Evan's insistence, she'd stuffed some old towels inside a box and set it on the fire escape to give them a bit of shelter from the cold. Sometimes, she had leftovers from the diner she set out for them. It was the closest thing to a pet the landlord allowed them to have.

"No leftovers tonight, sweetie." Corie folded up her work sweater and set it on the quilt beside her while she untied her shoes and toed them off her feet. Even through the blackout drapes that covered her window, she could hear how agitated the cat was, meowing and hissing and bumping into the discarded chair she'd set out there to anchor the box and keep it from blowing away. "What in the world are you so fired up about?"

Corie padded across the room in her stockinged feet. But before she reached the window, she heard another sound from out in the living room. A soft knocking at her door. Three taps, a pause, three more.

She glanced at the late hour on her alarm clock and tensed when she heard three more knocks. Hurrying straight to her coat on the rack where she'd hung it beside the door, she once more reached for her pepper spray.

Knock, knock, knock.

"Corie?"

Her breath rushed out in a gust of relief at Matt's deep-pitched whisper. She slipped the spray back into the pocket and swung open the door.

"You didn't lock your dead bolt. I was waiting—"

Corie threw her arms around Matt's neck. "Thank you. For so many things, thank you." Her toes left the floor as Matt wound his arms behind her waist and straightened, completing the hug. Her toes were still dangling in the air as she leaned back against his arms and grinned. "Ax-chopping contest? Seriously?"

"Oh. That." Her feet hit the floor and she was no longer cinched against him as he tried to apologize. "My brother and I were taking down a wall. Ev wasn't in the room at the time—"

"It sounds like a manly man thing that humans with testosterone enjoy more than they should. But I know he was safe. I feel safe with you, too—emotionally, physically." She shrugged, not coming up with enough words to explain everything she was feeling. "Firewise. Otherwise." She felt giddy, partially with relief that there was no intruder at her door, probably with fatigue, possibly because of all the new emotions swirling inside her. "I like you, Matt. I know my timing isn't great and inexplicable things are happening around us, but I do. Will I see you tomorrow?" she asked, wanting these weird, wonderful feelings she'd discovered tonight to continue.

He propped his hands at his waist and gave her the matter-of-fact answer she was getting used to. "I work the late shift. Won't get home until eight or nine."

The giddiness fled, and she felt deflated. "I'll be at work by then. Well, thank you again for watching Evan tonight. I promise I won't bug you every time I—"

His big hands framed her jaw, and his lips covered hers, silencing her apology with a kiss. He'd cut her off midsentence, and she was surprised to realize she was okay with that. Her gasp of surprise was swallowed up by the pressure of his mouth gliding over hers. Matt's tongue slipped between her lips, but she was already opening for him, already answering him. She was already grasping fistfuls of his shirt and T-shirt and the hard muscle underneath and pulling herself into his kiss.

Matt sifted his fingers into her hair and cupped her head, tilting it back to ravish her mouth. He moved forward, backing her against the wall beside the door until she could feel the pressure of his thighs against parts of her body that hadn't felt anything remotely thrilling like this for far too long. The heat of his body trapped her there, consuming her the way his mouth was consuming hers.

Although it had been a teasing joke earlier that night, Corie thought of molasses in the very best of ways. Matt's kiss was slow and smooth, addictively sweet and very much worth the wait for him to take the initiative in expressing his desire for her. Every taste, every exploration was as deliberate as his every thought.

But with a groan of regret that matched her own, Matt lifted his head, ending the kiss. They were both breathing erratically, the proud tips of her sensitized breasts brushing against his chest with every exhale. She was vaguely aware of his arousal pushing at the front of his jeans, just as she was aware of the heavy, weepy center of her wishing this had been more than a kiss. She had been too long without a man. She had been forever without the right man. Oh, how this man made her feel—physically, emotionally—every scary, delicious way she'd long forgotten she had the right to feel.

His dark eyes replaced the intensity of his kiss as he studied her face, keeping them linked together with his gaze. He watched her hair as he brushed his fingers through it, trying to smooth it back into place until he finally pulled the band from what was left of her ponytail and let her hair fall over her shoulders.

His voice was a husky whisper as he gently pried her hands from his shirt and slipped the rubber band into her palm. "I'll see you tomorrow night." She nodded at his promise because she couldn't quite find the breath to speak. "How late is the diner open?"

"On Fridays and Saturdays, we close at midnight."

"Evan?"

"He'll be with me. There's a cot in the back room if

he's not at one of the tables, drawing or playing or chatting with the regular customers."

With a nod, he released her entirely and backed away with his hands raised, making her feel like pure temptation despite her baby-blue polyester dress and messy hair. "I'll meet you guys there when my shift ends. You still owe me a pie."

She laughed out loud at that and clapped her hand over her mouth as the sound seemed to echo down the hallway. Matt smiled—just a small curve at one corner of his mouth transformed him into a handsome man. And those dark, coffee-colored eyes about swallowed her up. She reached up to rest her hand against the stubble on his jaw. "Good night, Matt."

"Good night, Corie." She drifted into her apartment and closed the door, leaning back against it. From the hallway, she heard him exhale and whisper, "Dead bolt."

Why did that reminder sound like some kind of endearment?

Corie quickly turned and threw the bolt, alleviating his concern. She splayed her hand against the door, imagining that his hand was there on the other side, protecting her, connecting them. Corie caught her abraded, swollen lip between her teeth and savored the taste of him that lingered there.

She had never in her life been kissed like that. She'd never before understood how a man could make every part of her tingle with such a sharp need with just a kiss. She'd never understood how freeing trust could be, never understood how hope and laughter could make falling in love so exciting.

Falling in love. Was that what was happening here? Was it foolish of her to want like this? To believe she was getting a second chance to be happy? To hope that Matt was feeling this way, too?

After a moment, she heard Matt's door open and close. It had been six long years since her divorce from Kenny, and this was the first time in all those years that she was looking forward to seeing a man again. She was looking forward to seeing Matt.

She heard the cat scrabbling down the fire escape steps as she pushed away from the door and headed through the apartment to get ready for bed herself and idly wondered what was making the feline so restless. Pulling the curtain aside, she peered out into the night. It was too dark to see much beyond the glass. The box beneath the chair had been knocked askew, and the snow around it had been disturbed enough that the paw prints were indistinct. Maybe there'd been one occupant too many trying to share the box tonight. Seeing no critter outside for her to worry about, Corie made sure the window was locked and pulled the drape back into place.

Kenny hadn't found them. She'd freaked out for nothing. Besides, she had more pleasant things to think about.

Like kissing Matt Taylor again.

Many, many times.

Chapter Nine

Matt pulled the steering wheel and hung a sharp left at just the right distance to avoid the cars parked against the curb, guiding the big fire engine onto the skinny side street beside the dubiously named KC's Best automotive repair shop off McGee Street. Talk about a dead man district. This was their third job of the day, and each fire had been bigger than the last. Counting the five medical calls to back up their EMTs, the cat that was stuck in a drainpipe and the two false alarms, Firehouse 13 was way above its daily call average.

After the engine hissed and squealed to a stop, Matt set the brakes and killed the siren. The red and blue flashing lights bounced off nearby shop windows and windshields but seemed to be absorbed by the swirling orange and yellow flames shooting out of the repair shop's garage doors. Inky smoke billowed skyward, staining the snow on the branches of the ancient oaks that lined the sidewalk and bringing an early night to the evening sky.

"Nice driving, Taylor." Captain Redding put on his white scene commander's helmet. "Mark, Jackson—

priority one is to make sure we don't have gas tanks, oxyacetylene canisters or other flammables on site that haven't already gone up. Remove them if we can. Clear a perimeter if we can't."

"Yes, sir," they answered, fastening up their gear and securing their air tanks in the back seat.

Redding glanced across the cab to Matt. "You co-ordinate with the utility crew to make sure we've got all the gas lines cut off. I'll track down the owner and talk to whoever reported it." He studied the fully engulfed building. "This was burning awhile before anyone called it in. As far as I know, Friday's still a workday. Why didn't anyone call sooner?"

"You think we've got casualties?" Matt asked.

"I'm thinking I don't want to send any more men in there than I have to. Something's off with this one." Redding made a quick scan of the police cars blocking traffic and the local residents hanging out at a relatively safe distance from the fire scene. "Where are all the me-chanics?" There was one nondescript guy with muscles and an aversion to holding his head up huddled inside his grimy insulated coveralls, talking with an older man in a suit and tie and long dress coat. "He's the only one in this crowd wearing a uniform of any kind."

Twenty-plus years of service gave Kyle Redding al-most a sixth sense about fires. Hell. Matt hadn't been with KCFD for half that long, and he had a feeling there was nothing accidental about this blaze. Matt nodded toward the line of tow trucks and trailers on the far side of the building holding expensive cars and souped-up trucks in various states of repair. "Looks like they got most of their vehicles out."

"The ones worth some real money." Redding nodded. "Which is what I would do if I was going to torch my own place."

Matt followed up on Kyle's suspicion. "I'll give my dad a call and alert the arson team."

"Do that."

While the captain led Mark, Ray and the rest of the team off the truck to meet with the men and women on the second and third trucks and move them into position, Matt turned off the engine and called in their twenty to dispatch. "Lucky 13 on scene, 819 McGee Street. Captain Redding has the command. Taylor 13 Alpha out."

Then he swapped out his ball cap for his own helmet and tuned in to the chatter coming over his body radio as he climbed down to assess the scene more closely. The heat from the blaze was intense enough for him to feel it as he approached. Although hoses were out and the team was laying down a defensive perimeter to keep the fire from spreading, there was probably little they could do.

Matt adjusted his mask over his face, radioed his position to the crew and moved inside, clinging to the walls to keep his bearings as he tried to pinpoint the source of the blaze. Steam from the water gushing through the garage bay doors was as thick as the smoke, making visibility almost nil. After signaling Mark and Ray that he understood their all-clear on the ground floor, he made his way past the charred shell of a pickup up on lifts in one of the bays. A quick exploration confirmed that no one was trapped inside or beneath the vehicle. He made it to a set of metal stairs leading up to the second floor. But he was forced to reverse course as flames curled in a sinuous dance across the ceiling above him and cut off access to the top of the stairs. One by one, ceiling tiles melted and fell away, and the wood support beams holding up the second floor began to sag and crack as fire, water and heat weakened them. The thick stone walls and iron window frames would probably survive anything short of a massive explosion, but the interior of the two-story 1920s-era shop was fully involved and about to collapse.

"Taylor 13 Alpha," he called over his radio. "Everybody clear out. The top floor's about to rain down on us. Immediate source of ignition not evident. Cannot access second floor from interior. I repeat, everybody clear out."

Mark and Ray were already outside, waiting for the ladder truck to move into position to access the roof when Matt emerged. His mask fogged up as he met the wintry air and he pulled it down beneath his chin.

"Incendiaries down here are contained," Mark shouted. "The ignition point has to be upstairs."

He gave them a thumbs-up, showing his understanding. "Did you see the way the interior supports were burning? It's like somebody doused the top floor with an accelerant. This baby is going to end up a total gut. All we can do now is put it out." Matt tapped his radio, indicating to the crew that this had become strictly a containment mission. "Lucky 13, let's go to work. Watch yourselves up on that roof."

Matt was heading across the driveway to report to Captain Redding when a window exploded over his head. He jerked at the sound and instinctively raised his arm as glass rained down around him. But that was what the helmet and bunker gear were for, since falling debris and collapsing buildings were a firefighter's most common threat. Unharmed, he moved his mask up to shield his face, and looked up to see if the pressure that had blown out that window was the first in a chain reaction, and he needed to move his men back to a safe distance. Flashover would certainly occur now that fresh oxygen was flooding the confined space.

"Son of a…" What Matt saw was even worse. "Stop!"

A dark-haired man in grimy coveralls was leaning over the window ledge, engulfed by the black smoke billowing out around him. Coughing racked his body, and when he drew in a breath, Matt could hear the shallow wheeze of lungs that wouldn't fill. His face was smudged with soot and red smears he'd guess were blood, making his expression unreadable. But there was no mistaking his intention as the chair he'd smashed the window with came flying toward Matt.

Matt ran forward, dodging the chair that splintered around him, shouting to be heard over the roar of the fire and thunder of the hoses. A leg came over the edge of the windowsill. "Wait up! We'll get a ladder to you. Stop! Take a deep breath and stay put. We're coming." He waved the man back inside, pointed to the fire escape at the end of the building. "Can you reach—?"

Matt turned to his radio. "Ladder! Northeast side, second floor. I've got a jumper—"

The man teetered over the edge into the smoke, leaping, falling, hurling himself away from the flames. Matt dived in one Hail Mary effort to break his fall. But he was too late. The victim hit the pavement before him with a sickening thud.

On his hands and knees, Matt scrambled forward. "Medic! I need a board now!"

Matt tugged off his mask and placed it over the man's face, giving him the oxygen he must have been starving for. He peeled off his gloves to check for a pulse. But as the EMTs swarmed in and pushed him aside, he already knew the diagnosis. Whether it was a broken neck or a broken skull, the man was dead.

Matt rocked back on his heels as Redding rushed over. Although the paramedics rolled the mechanic onto a back board to stabilize him and intubated him to push oxygen directly into his lungs, it was too late. After giving Matt's shoulder a supportive squeeze, the captain knelt beside the paramedics. "I think I understand now why someone started this fire."

Matt scrambled over to join him, needing to know why this man had died, needing to understand why he hadn't been able to save him. Faulty fire suppression system? Not passing any fire inspection period? What the hell kind of business left a man behind without making any effort to rescue him, or alerting the KCFD to attempt a rescue? "Did you find out anything from the owner?"

"That he's an entitled ass full of hot air. But take a

look at this." After a sad shake of his head from one of the EMTs working on the victim, Redding picked up the man's wrist and pushed back the cuff of his cover-alls. The man's fingers and knuckles were bruised and bloodied, like he'd been in a fight. Matt might have thought the fight had been with the heavy iron and leaded glass of that window upstairs, but that didn't account for the shred of duct tape clinging to his wrist.

Before the medics covered him up, Matt glimpsed the dark-haired man's bruised and swollen face. He'd clearly been in a fight. "Those wounds are hours old. They didn't happen when he impacted the concrete." Matt picked up the other wrist and discovered the skin was raw from where he'd pulled or gnawed his way free. "He didn't bind himself up like this."

"Crime scene cover-up." Redding placed the victim's hand back under the blanket and nodded for the EMTs to lift him onto the gurney and move him to the ambulance, keeping him out of sight from curious on-lookers and the press photographers who were showing up to take pictures or capture some footage for the evening news. "Somebody left this man for dead in there."

"Hold up a sec." Matt asked the medics to wait while he took another look at the man's damaged wrist.

The captain leaned in beside him. "What is that? A homemade tattoo?"

Matt studied the markings that looked like they'd been scratched into the skin by the same instrument the man had used to free himself. Suspicion prickled the back of Matt's neck, and he wiped the soot away from the patch sewn above the man's chest pocket to read his name. "Maldonado." The man whose car had been remotely set on fire a few days ago. The confidential informant who was allegedly ratting out the next generation of the Meade crime family. "My uncle Cole needs to see this."

Redding ordered the medics to stay with the body and protect it. "I'll call KCPD."

Two hours later, night had fallen, and with the fire out, the temperature had dropped to a chilly twenty-three degrees. And while the Lucky 13 crew was combing the building to check for remaining hot spots and overhaul the debris, KCPD had arrived on the scene in the form of Matt's uncle Cole, along with his NCIS partner, Amos Rand.

Matt was running on fumes, taking a break and sitting on the running board of his fire truck while he downed a bottle of water. Other than removing his helmet and breathing apparatus, he still wore his bunker gear for the warmth the layers provided. He stood when his uncle and his partner walked up, extending his hand to greet them. "Uncle Cole. Agent Rand."

"Matt." Cole held on to his nephew's hand for an extra moment, his eyes narrowed in familial concern. "You look like you've been rode hard and put up wet. You okay?"

"Long day."

Cole nodded his understanding. Sometimes, first responders saw some wicked things that stuck with you—like a man desperate enough to choose one kind of death over another. "I'll need your statement when you're ready."

"Let's get it done." Matt crushed the empty water bottle and tossed it inside the truck. He told them what he'd witnessed with Enrique Maldonado's death and his suspicion about the cause of the fire. There was only one worker on site besides the dead man, and he hadn't seen that first mechanic since he'd had time to walk away from the fire and scan the crowd again. Finally, someone had managed to save all the expensive vehicles they had on site—but not their last employee?

"Sounds like potential insurance fraud to me," Cole suggested.

Amos agreed. "Maybe Meade needed an influx of cash and decided to torch his own place."

"Or he was destroying evidence." Matt nodded toward the forensics team from the crime lab who'd been talking to Cole and Amos. "Has your crime scene team found anything?"

Amos pulled his wool cap more securely over his buzz cut of hair and hunched against the damp chill in the air. "They can't get into what's left of the offices upstairs yet, but they found a sticky substance on the arm of the chair Maldonado used to break out the window. They'll have to match it in the lab, but it looks like remnants of duct tape. He was secured to the chair and worked over before the fire started. Trapped and unable to evacuate. Maybe he was unconscious—maybe they thought he was dead. Nobody tried to save that guy."

Somebody had. But it had been too little, too late. Matt heard the sound of the victim hitting the pavement again and again in his head. "If I could have just gotten to him sooner. If I had known he was up there—"

"This isn't on you, Matt," Cole insisted. Captain Redding had said the same thing, ordered him to take tomorrow off and to check in with one of the KCFD counselors, if necessary. "Whether as a result of another crime like arson or assault, or deliberately planned to play out like this, we've got ourselves a homicide. One we should be able to tie to the owner of this place, Chad Meade."

Amos turned his back to the graying, slightly heavyset man in the suit and tie being escorted by a uniformed officer across the driveway to join them. "Speak of the devil."

Although Matt had spotted him in the crowd with the missing mechanic when the Lucky 13 crew had first arrived on the scene, he hadn't realized this well-to-do man who wore polished patent-leather oxfords instead of sensible snow boots was the business owner. He didn't strike Matt as an auto repair sort of guy. But then, he didn't look like Matt's image of a man who'd spent several years in prison, either. But this was Chad Meade, wannabe crime boss and the object of Cole and Amos's investigation.

"If it isn't Mr. Taylor and his enigmatic partner," Meade said in a friendly enough tone, although Matt got the distinct impression there was nothing friendly between him and the police. "We meet again. I was told you wanted to speak to me and, of course, I was eager to help find out who is responsible for this monstrous tragedy. Thought I could spare you a few minutes between phone calls and press interviews." He held up the cell phone he carried. "I've been talking back and forth with my insurance gal. I'm guessing this will be a total write-off." He glanced up at Matt and gave a practiced laugh. "These old buildings from the '20s are built like bomb shelters on the outside. But KCFD couldn't save much on the inside, could they?"

Cole made no pretensions of this being a civil conversation. "How much of a profit is this *write-off* worth to you, Chad? Aren't you on parole?"

He turned the collar of his coat up against the cold. "That's why I'm running a legitimate business here, Officer."

"It's Detective."

Amos removed the toothpick that he'd been chewing from the side of his mouth and tapped his chest. "And Special Agent. *You* need to try harder if you want us to believe you've gone legit."

Meade pointed to the smoking wreckage of the garage. "Can I help it if the competition doesn't want me to succeed?"

"You're claiming this was a setup?" Cole challenged.

"I have enemies, Detective. My uncle Jericho was an influential man—not everyone agreed with the way he ran his business. I've learned from the mistakes he made and I'm doing well for myself. But some people can hold a grudge for a long time." He pulled back the edge of his leather glove to check the time, as if he was calculating how much longer he'd allow this conversation to last. "You, perhaps. How is your lovely wife, by the way?"

"I'm here to do my job, Meade." Cole clearly had no intention of letting Chad Meade bait him into an argument about the last time Cole and his wife, Tori, had investigated the Meade crime family. "You've got a casualty here. One of your employees, Enrique Maldonado. He was trapped in the fire. He didn't make it."

"I heard. That's too bad."

Matt's hand balled into a fist at the lack of sympathy, or even empathy, for the life that had been lost.

Cole nodded. "Yeah, it's too bad he had his hands taped together and was probably unconscious when the fire started and had no chance of surviving."

Chad Meade met Cole's hard, unblinking blue eyes and finally smiled before looking away. Since members of Chad's family had once tried to kill Cole's wife, there was certainly no love lost between them. "I know nothing about that, Detective Taylor. But I assure you, the company takes care of its employees and their families. Now, if you'll excuse me, I need to talk to my insurance people and do a little PR spin with the press." He gestured to the burned-out shell of the garage. "Historic landmark destroyed. It breaks the locals' hearts."

Cole shoved his hands into his leather jacket, probably hiding the fists he'd made, too. "We'll be investigating this fire for arson. Maybe you think we can't get you for murder, but even a case of insurance fraud will put you back in prison."

"I'm just the investor who owns the property. An entrepreneur. What would I know about setting a fire like this?" He wiggled his gloved fingers in the air. "I don't even smoke anymore." He turned and waved to a brunette reporter who waved back and invited him to speak on camera. "Gentlemen. If you'll excuse me, I have to go."

Amos followed a few steps behind him. "We have more questions for you, Meade."

"I'm certain you do." Despite his perfect, capped-tooth smile, Meade's tone was laced with a threat now. "I'm not in the business anymore, gentlemen. And your investigation borders on harassment."

Cole was one cool customer, throwing Meade's excuse right back at him. "If you're not in the business, then you've got nothing to hide."

Chad Meade smoothed his tie inside his suit jacket before reaching into the chest pocket of his coat. "But I *do* have work to do, calls to make. A family to express my condolences to." He held out a business card. "If you want to speak to me again, contact my lawyer."

Amos snagged the card and stuffed it into the back pocket of his jeans as Meade strolled away. "That man is one smug SOB. He does know we've built a paper trail on him, doesn't he? That we can track his import and export shipment schedules to match up with trafficking in and out of KCI and the river port? What we need is witness corroboration. Several witnesses would be better."

Cole shook his head. "Now that Maldonado's gone, we'll be starting from scratch again, trying to convince someone to turn on Meade." His expression was grim as he looked to the blackened shell of the Art Deco building. "But if this is the result of turning on him…"

Matt listened to their case against Chad Meade, and a few inexplicable observations about this fire began to make sense. "Can I show you something?" The three men went to the body lying in the back of the ME's van. Cole and Amos flashed the badges hanging around their necks and vouched for Matt as a witness. With permission from the medical examiner, Niall Watson, who remained to observe their interactions with the body, the three men climbed in beside the gurney. Dr. Watson issued them all sterile gloves and proceeded to unzip the body bag.

"Can you identify the victim?" Dr. Watson asked, adjusting his glasses on the bridge of his nose. "I found no ID on him. No wallet, no phone."

"It's Enrique Maldonado," Amos confirmed. "May I?" Amos pulled a knife from the sheath on his belt and slid it beneath the top of the victim's boot. Once he'd pried it far enough from the victim's leg, he reached inside and pulled out a set of dog tags on a thin chain. He dropped the tags into a bag the ME held open before sealing and labeling it. "Perps don't usually check the boot for anything but hidden weapons. Those will confirm his ID. Maldonado was working undercover for me out of NCIS. We believe Meade has his hand in moving illegal arms in and out of the country by hiding them in those expensive cars he imports and exports. Enrique was our inside man who followed the trail here to Kansas City." Amos's light-colored eyes narrowed as he looked down at the body. "He was a good man. He wasn't even a field agent, but we gave him the job because he's so good with engines and cars. No one would question his expertise."

Cole rested a hand on Amos's shoulder. "Sorry about your man, Amos."

"He was a good Marine." The dark-haired agent closed his eyes completely for a moment, inhaled a deep breath, then opened his eyes, ready to work again. "He's been feeding us intel for months now. We still don't know if Meade is running this operation, or if he's a middleman and we still have to identify who he's reporting to."

Cole studied the victim's battered face for a moment before looking away. "Burning his car wasn't persuasion enough to keep Maldonado from meeting with us. Was his cover blown and Meade found out he was a cop? Or is this the going payback for anyone talking to the police now?"

Matt had an idea about that. "If Maldonado was working for you, that could explain what I found." He lifted the stiff left arm from the gurney and pulled back the stained, torn sleeve. "I thought you might want to see this." Dr. Watson snapped a photograph of Maldonado's forearm, and the letters and number that had literally been scratched into his skin.

N4 Jeff C FB

Cole pulled out his phone and took a picture of the code. "You think he did this? Or was it done to him?"

Matt laid the arm down and picked up the victim's right hand to show them the bloody nails. "With everything on fire around him, and nothing to write with, he carved this himself." Cole and the ME both snapped pictures of the hand, as well. "I think he jumped because he wanted to make sure you got his message. I can't be certain what it means, but it looks like he was trying to preserve the writing in case his clothes caught on fire and the body burned."

"N4. Enforcer," Amos translated. "Jeff C? Jefferson City? Meade's hired himself a new enforcer from Jefferson City. Probably an ex-con who just got out of prison there."

Ex-con? Like Corie's ex?

"Is that why the call from your attorney's office upset you?"

"My ex hurt a lot of people."

The back of Matt's neck prickled with awareness. He glanced outside the ME's van at his crewmates finishing their cleanup and joking with each other now that the danger at this scene had passed. He stepped to the edge of the van to look at the gathering of reporters and cameras closing in around Chad Meade. But he wasn't sure what his instincts were trying to tell him.

"What's the FB?" Cole asked.

Matt glanced back to see Amos scraping some goo off the bottom of the dead man's boot. "Looks like petroleum jelly." He showed it to the ME, who opened a jar for him to scrape the substance into.

What details was Matt missing here? "May I?"

He brought the jar to his nose to sniff the contents. Oh no. Hell no.

"You ever seen anything like that?" Cole asked.

Matt had. His blood sped through his veins like a freight train.

Corie said her ex started fires.

"Kenny stayed in Jefferson City after he was released from prison."

That's why the hairs on the back of his neck were standing out straight. He handed the jar back to the ME, who capped it as evidence. "Get another sample of that to my dad, chief arson investigator at KCFD." Matt jumped from the back of the van to the ground. "You need me for anything else, Cole? There's a phone call I need to make." The sooner the crew cleared the scene and he wrote up his preliminary report, the sooner he could get to Pearl's Diner and to Corie and Evan. But all that would wait if he couldn't hear her voice and know that she was okay.

"Go." His uncle shooed him on his way. "I'll contact Gideon about the potential arson. Thanks for your help tonight. I'll keep you in the loop if we find out anything about the fire itself."

Matt was backing away, even as he was unbuckling his turnout coat and reaching inside his BDUs to pull out his cell phone. He nodded toward the victim Niall Watson was zipping back inside the body bag. "FB. Firebug. Check out the name Kenny Norwell. Find out if he's got any connection to Chad Meade. And send me Norwell's picture if you can get it."

"Done." Cole called after him, "Who's Norwell?"

"Someone I hope is still in Jefferson City."

Chapter Ten

"Answer your phone!" Matt growled the order at the cell phone he'd anchored to his dashboard.

When Corie's voice mail started up again with its pleasant but impersonal greeting, he punched the disconnect button. He'd already left three messages, apologizing for running late, asking her to call him, telling her he had some information he wanted to share in person, trying not to sound completely desperate to know that she was okay.

He'd had to settle for a single text.

Hey, Matt. We're slammed tonight. Call you back when things lighten up.

At least if she was super busy, she wasn't alone. And he couldn't imagine any universe where she didn't make sure Evan was safe, as well. They were probably fine, and he was too exhausted by the day and his anticipation at seeing her beautiful smile again to be able to filter out the negative thoughts.

He forced himself to take a deep breath and slow to a stop for the red light at the next intersection.

He had no proof that her ex-husband was in Kansas City, breaking into her apartment, setting small fires around their building and killing undercover agents. Uncle Cole had texted him a copy of Kenneth Norwell's mugshot. A man could change his looks a lot in six years—grow a beard, shave his head or dye his hair or let it grow long. Still, Matt had memorized the image and had wearied his brain trying to recall if he'd seen anyone like that around Corie and Evan. If he'd seen anyone like that in the crowds of lookie-loos at any of the area's recent suspicious fires. But he'd been focused on doing his job—putting out the flames, not spotting the man who may have started them.

Cole had also shared that Norwell's residence was in Jefferson City. His parole officer confirmed that Norwell had been at every check-in since his release. Still, Jeff City was only a two-and-a-half-hour drive from KC. Close enough to get to Kansas City to set a fire and get back in time for his required daily meetings. But did that put him in the city long enough to play games with Corie's sense of security? Did that give him time to drive to St. Louis to torch an attorney's office to find her new name and address in the first place?

Someone was conducting a harassment campaign against Corie and her son. Someone wanted her to be unsettled and afraid, possibly to distract her enough to drop her guard so she wouldn't see the big threat coming—and maybe just because some sicko got off on gaslighting her and seeing her afraid. And there

was no denying that someone had started those fires
at their building with a flammable goo that bore a re-
markable resemblance to the accelerant used to burn
down Chad Meade's pricey automotive repair place.

It could all be a tragic coincidence. Or it could be
that Corie's violent past had come back to haunt her in
the worst of ways.

Matt drummed his fingers against the steering
wheel, counting down the seconds until the light turned
green and the car ahead of him pulled out. He had a
portable siren and flashing lights in his truck he could
turn on to cut through traffic faster, but the only justi-
fiable emergency was the worst-case scenario playing
through his head and twisting at his heart. And as far
as he knew, that hadn't happened yet.

Plus, Corie and Evan weren't the only citizens he was
responsible for here. An arsonist in Kansas City? An
uptick in the number of fire calls KCFD had answered
in the past month—everything from the woman this
morning who had accidentally ignited a pile of laundry
when she tried to light her water heater to the gut job
at Meade's automotive shop this evening—were cause
for concern that no one should be ignoring. Not every
fire was arson, but every fire was dangerous—and a
potential killer, even if you hadn't been bound up and
left for dead in the middle of one.

Unfortunately, it was a single-digit Friday night during the long haul of January, and the bars and eateries
around the City Market were open and doing a booming
business. There were dozens of patrons hurrying along
the sidewalks, getting in and out of cars and buses and

cabs, and hundreds more were already inside, staying warm while they flirted and partied and filled their bellies with food and drink. Every one of them could be at risk if Kenny Norwell was in town, setting fires for whoever paid him the right price.

Matt tapped on the accelerator as the light changed. "Don't project the worst."

But the tension cording the back of his neck warned him that the worst was yet to happen.

He turned the corner and spotted the familiar neon sign and bright light from the interior spilling through the big glass windows of Pearl's Diner at the far end of the block. But he was too far away to see inside, to spot Corie's bouncing ponytail or Evan's shaggy brown hair. Parking was going to be a bear around here, and he vowed then and there to pull into the first available parking space he came across that would fit his big truck, and then he'd run the rest of the way to the diner. He'd told Corie he'd get off by eight or nine, and it was half past ten. In the past, he hadn't minded the responsibilities he enjoyed as a lieutenant at Firehouse 13. But tonight, every frozen hose, every incident report that needed at least a preliminary summary, every offer of support and camaraderie from his crewmates over that last rough call had taken precious time away from getting to Corie and Evan. Even the twenty minutes he'd stopped to shower the smells of soot and death off him and change into jeans and a sweater had taken too long.

Now he was circling the block for a second time, seriously rethinking turning on his flashing lights and double parking outside the diner's front door, all because he wasn't good at putting his thoughts into words. He wasn't sure he could express his fears about Norwell finding a way to track down Corie and Evan's new names and showing up on their doorstep again without Matt sounding like he was barking out orders and scaring her.

Especially if this turned out to be nothing. Maybe the fires were accidents. Maybe Chad Meade had killed Agent Rand's man himself. And maybe this gut-deep edginess had less to do with arson fires and more to do with the feelings he had for Corie that were bottled up inside him.

His phone rang on the dash. When he saw the name on the screen, it didn't ring a second time.

Matt pushed the button to answer the call. "Corie."

Not Corie. He heard noises in the background, some garbled talking, the clink of dishes and silverware, a couple of raised voices, but nothing he could make out.

"Matt?" Evan's voice sounded small and nasally. Was he crying? "Is it okay if I call you?"

"Sure, bud." Matt's heart lurched in his chest. Was something wrong? Was that why Corie hadn't called him back? He ratcheted down the tension that threatened to leak into his voice. "Are you okay? What are you doing on your mom's phone?"

"Mom needs help."

"What's wrong?"

He heard a big sniffle, and then Evan's voice grew stronger. "The customers are being mean to her." Customers. Plural. So probably not Norwell. Surely Evan would recognize his own father. But then, he would only have been one or two when Norwell went to prison. Corie would know him, though. Would she let on to Evan that it was his father? Maybe her ex wasn't even in town, and the fires at their building were just a co-incidence that overlapped Uncle Cole's investigation into Chad Meade's resurgence in organized crime and arms smuggling, and whatever was going on at the diner had nothing to do with the information he'd learned this evening.

Maybe someone had been rude about their service or had stiffed Corie on her tip. Maybe the kid took umbrage with that. Matt knew he would. But he kept his tone even and reassuring. "Not everybody is nice, Ev."

"They broke my dragon."

The night turned red behind Matt's eyes, and he bit down on the urge to curse where Evan could hear him. That plastic dragon was just a toy. But that toy clearly had emotional value to Evan. Heck, the kid literally swore by that dragon. Breaking it would damage more than the toy. It was a security blanket for Corie's son who'd grown up without a father. And damn it, it was Evan's.

"Some bullies aren't nice at all."

"The man with the beard said he was going to eat some of my bricks, but I think he hid them in his gross beard or his mashed potatoes. You can't eat plastic bricks. Mom's trying to make him give them back."

Hence the raised voices. "Is he hurting your mom?"

"I don't think so. But they're loud."

Finally. Another pickup was pulling out of a parking space across the street about half a block up from the diner. About damn time. "How many mean customers are there?"

"Two."

Gross beard? "There's the guy with the beard. What does the other man look like?"

"He has red hair and more freckles than I do."

Those jackasses from the bus. He remembered their names—Harve and Jordy. It took a lot to trigger Matt's temper. But with Maldonado's death, one too many arson fires, the possibility of Corie's ex working with Chad Meade and some stupid, drunk hicks hitting on Corie and breaking Evan's dragon, there just wasn't enough calm left in him to control his rage. "Did either of those men touch her?"

"Um…" Hell. They had. They'd put their hands on her.

Matt slammed on his brakes and angled his truck across the lane of traffic, staking claim to the parking space the moment the young couple climbing in left. "Is she okay? Are you?"

"Uh-huh."

"Do you dragon swear?"

He could almost hear the energy flowing into Evan's tone, and the confidence puffing up his chest. "Yes. I'm okay. Mom said to call you to see when you were coming before she called the police. When are you coming?"

"I'm parking my truck now."

"The red-haired guy asked Mom if her boyfriend was going to save her this time." The sound of fear in Evan's voice eased a little as curiosity kicked in. "What does that mean? Are you her boyfriend?"

"Damn straight I am." Matt whipped into the parking space. "Hang up the phone and tell your mom I'm coming."

"Mo-om!"

Then there was no more call. Matt grabbed his cell off the dash, pocketed his keys, put a hand up to stop the car bearing down on him and jogged across the street. Thanks to the diner's booth-to-ceiling windows, Matt had a clear view of what was happening before he ever reached the front door at the corner.

Harve and Jordy were easy to spot at their table in the middle of the restaurant with their mountain-man hygiene and penchant for making a scene. Neither one could be mistaken for the man in the mugshot of Kenny Norwell.

That didn't make the scene any easier to dismiss. Matt saw a wingless plastic dragon and brightly colored blocks scattered across the table and plate in front of Harve. Despite Evan's red-rimmed eyes, he sassed something to the bearded man and grabbed his dragon. When Harve shoved Evan away from the table, Corie dropped her empty tray and scooted Evan behind her, lambasting the bearded man. Matt lengthened his stride when he hit the sidewalk in front of Pearl's, running the last few yards.

A pregnant woman in a business suit stood at the front register, on her cell, reporting everything she was seeing, hopefully on the phone to 9-1-1. One older gentleman stood up at his table in the booth opposite Harve and Jordy and the McGuires, pointing a finger at the two men and rebuking them. That earned him

Jordy jumping up and shouting "Boo" or some other startling word that sent him tumbling back into his seat beside a white-haired woman. The rest of the customers watched the scene with wide-eyed shock or buried their gazes in their menus and plates, trying desperately not to get involved.

Involved was the call of every Taylor. Step up when someone needs help. Matt might not be a Taylor by blood. But he was a Taylor down to his very bones.

He swung the door open.

"It's one thing to get handsy with the waitstaff or harass a nice gentleman like Mr. Wallace," he heard Corie chide. "But you touch my son…"

The tinkling bell that jingled overhead sounded inordinately loud and somehow menacing in the sudden silence from every table. Matt made no effort to hunch his shoulders or tone down his anger. He knew how to make his presence known. Big dude at the front door. Black stocking cap, black jeans, black coat. Spooky quiet. Barely breathing hard despite a run through the cold night air. Dark eyes lasered in on the freckled hand clamped around Corie's forearm. Long, purposeful strides took him right up to the table where Harve Gross Beard and Jordy Freckle Face were harassing Corie and Evan.

"Well, if it ain't the boyfriend." Jordy announced Matt's arrival like a rehearsed line. "The boy said you'd show up tonight." But he glanced nervously across the table at Harve, unsure how to proceed.

Matt could help with that. "Let her go."

Although the younger man's grip instantly popped

open, Harve chuckled, urging his friend not to panic. "This is all a misunderstanding. The waitress just brought us our pie. We're gonna sit and enjoy dessert."

"No." Simple. Succinct.

Harve fisted his hands against his thighs and Jordy shifted to the edge of his seat. Both were dead give-aways to the two men's intentions.

Matt Taylor had a brother who was a highly trained SWAT cop. Another was a street patrolman who handled a K-9 partner. Hell, he'd grown up with three brothers. He knew what to do in a fight.

Not that this would be much of one.

When Harve shoved his chair back from the table, Matt toed the edge of the hard plastic tray on the floor, tipped it up into his hand and whacked the bearded man across the face, knocking him back onto his seat. Without wasting any movement, he jerked Harve's coat down his arms, twisting the sleeves and cinching them together behind the back of his chair. Jordy jumped to his feet and cocked his arm back to take a swing at Matt.

He heard Corie's shriek of a warning, raised his arm to deflect the blow and twisted to plant his fist in the middle of the red-haired man's solar plexus, stunning him. Before Jordy could catch his breath or yell uncle, Matt had pinned his arm behind his back and shoved his face down into his roast beef sandwich. When Harve tried to wriggle his chair back to kick out at him, Matt stomped his big boot down on his foot. The man yelped in pain and shouted for someone to call the cops, that he and his buddy were being assaulted by some bigfoot wild man. Matt was peripherally aware of a few customers snapping pictures of the altercation with their phones, but no one was calling anybody to help these two.

While Harve moaned in pain, Matt leaned over the man he had pinned to the table. "You two need to pick on somebody your own size. Not a little boy."

"We were just havin' some fun," Jordy argued. "He knows we were playin'." He turned toward Evan. "Right, kid?"

Corie hugged Evan closer to her side as the brave little man answered. "You're a bully! Bullies get sent to the office."

Matt twisted Jordy's arm a little harder, his eyes telling Harve he would do the same to him if he tried anything else. "Return everything you took from this boy. Now." With a nod to Corie, she loosened Harve's coat sleeves so he could free his hands before she backed away to hug Evan to her side again. Harve emptied his shirt pocket and dumped the plastic bricks on the tabletop. "All of them," Matt ordered.

Muttering a curse under his breath, Mr. Gross Beard dipped his fingers into the mashed potatoes on his plate and dug out three more pieces. When Matt raised an eyebrow, he dropped the pieces into his glass of water and swished them around to get most of the food off them. Then he fished them out with his spoon and put all of them in a napkin he handed to Corie. "Sorry, ma'am."

Corie took the napkin and guided Evan back to the last booth where the body of his dragon now sat. She settled her son into his seat and urged him to start rebuilding his toy.

"Mister," Jordy whined. "You gotta let me up. You're killin' me here."

No. He'd seen killing today. This was just a friendly conversation among three men who were about to reach an understanding. "Are you going to touch this woman again?"

"C'mon. She's pretty. I just wanted her attention. She smiled at everybody but us—" Matt applied the slightest of pressure to his wrist. "No. No, sir."

"Are you going to harass her or anyone else in this restaurant?"

There were no excuses this time. "No, sir."

Matt released his grip and stepped back, making sure Corie and Evan were behind him, and there was a clear aisle to the front door. "Get out."

Jordy eagerly grabbed his coat and booked it to the front door. Harve was slower to rise to his feet and adjust his jacket onto his shoulders with a firm snap of the material. His eye contact seemed to say that this *conversation* wasn't over. "You don't know who you're messin' with, *Boyfriend.*"

Matt didn't take kindly to a threat like that. "Neither do you."

Eventually, Harve, too, backed away from Matt and headed for the door.

The entire diner seemed to be holding its collective breath as the bearded man stopped at the hostess stand and pulled out a wad of cash in his money clip.

"I don't want your money." The dark-haired woman cradled one hand protectively over her swollen belly and held her cell phone up and snapped a picture. "You two aren't welcome here anymore. If you come in again, I'll call one of my close connections at KCPD—like my husband." She put the phone back to her ear. "I'm texting you the second man's picture now, hon. Uh-huh." She held out the phone again. "Detective Kincaid would like to speak to you."

"Harve, come on." Jordy waited in the open door, letting the cold air rush in and chill the air. "One of them dates Bigfoot? And the other's married to a cop? I don't care how good the money is, we're out of our league—"

"Shut up."

"I know you said we owe—"

"Move!" Harve shoved Jordy outside. The bell above the door dinged as the door finally closed behind them.

How good the money is? Was somebody paying those two to harass Corie?

He had a sick idea of who that might be.

Before they reached the curb, Harve was on his phone texting someone. Matt stood at the window and watched, waiting for them to leave, not just the diner, but the whole neighborhood. After Harve put away his phone, he glanced back at Matt and offered him a mocking salute. Then the light changed, and Jordy pulled his seething partner along with the group of people crossing the street. A dark muscle car with tinted windows screeched to a stop at the far curb and the two men climbed inside. Harve must have texted for the ride to pick them up. But that was no car service to arrive this fast. That had to be a buddy of theirs, waiting close by. Maybe close enough to have watched the confrontation through the diner windows.

Matt glanced down at the license plate and committed it to memory. But he made no effort to call it in until he was certain that the yahoo twins and their unseen chauffeur had driven away. Then he quickly texted the plate number to Cole and asked him to ID the vehicle owner and possibly find out Harve and Jordan's last names.

Finally exhaling a sigh of relief that the incident was over, Matt exchanged a nod with the woman at the hostess stand, now fully engaged in a conversation with her husband, who was no doubt feeling just as worried and far away from where he needed to be as Matt had felt a few minutes earlier. Only then did he turn to Corie. "Are you two...?" Corie launched herself at Matt, throwing her arms around him while Evan latched onto his waist in between them. Funny how much better he felt now, too. "Okay."

The elderly gentleman who'd tried to help led the applause. Matt wound one arm around Corie and kissed the crown of her hair, inhaling the homey, enticing scent of baked goods, hard work and fruity shampoo that was hers alone. He palmed the back of Evan's head and held them both close, strengthened by the needy, welcoming grasp of their hands, loving the sense of completeness he felt at holding mother and son in his arms.

After introducing himself and making sure the older gentleman was okay, Matt thanked him for attempting to intervene. Mr. Wallace sat down, and he and the other patrons returned to their meals and conversations. Corie fisted a hand in Matt's coat and stretched up on tiptoe to press a kiss to the edge of Matt's jaw. "Thank you. I know I keep saying that but, thank you."

Every nerve ending in Matt's body zinged to the imprint where her soft lips had grazed his skin. The adrenaline that had spurred him into the diner was pulsing erratically through his system now, his hyperalertness to all things McGuire now warring with the bone-deep weariness from the day. He needed to keep it together for a while longer, trade some information, ensure they were safe—or there'd be no rest sufficient to help him recover from losing them. "Did they hurt you or Evan?"

"No."

He tipped Evan's head up to his and winked. "You dragon swear you're okay?" Evan grinned at Matt's understanding of the boy's highest code of honor. Evan crossed his finger over his heart and nodded before running back to his booth like the happy child he should be to start building again.

With Evan gone, Corie moved her arms to Matt's waist and snuggled closer. "I dragon swear, too," she teased. "But I'm not too proud to admit that I've never been happier to see anyone in my whole life. I knew when those two walked in and asked to be seated in my section that there was going to be trouble." With an angry huff, she pulled away, but only to move to his side and hug herself around his arm, turning toward the last booth by the windows where Evan was playing. "What kind of man gets rough with a child like that? Steals from him like it's some kind of joke?"

"No kind of *man*." Matt leaned over and kissed the crown of her hair. "I figured Evan would be safe with

you here. But I was scared at how far you might go to protect him."

She shook her head. "I got another waitress to cover the table for me, thinking if I wasn't there to entertain them, they'd eat fast and leave. But when they approached Evan, I had to step in." She rubbed her cheek against Matt's coat sleeve. "Of course, I know they only did it to get me to react. But it was nice to know I had backup before I charged in to do battle."

He covered both her hands with his. "I will always be here if you need me. I'm glad you called."

The pregnant boss lady had circled around the middle tables and met them near the back booth. She extended her hand to Matt. "I'm Melissa Kincaid. I run Pearl's Diner. Your meal is on the house."

"Matt Taylor. I appreciate you calling the police." Although he shook her hand, he shrugged off her offer. "I just want coffee and a slice of pie."

"Still on the house." She held up her phone before tucking into the pocket of her jacket. "And don't worry about Corie's safety when she's here. After the story I just told my husband, Sawyer, I imagine half of KCPD will be eating their meals here the rest of the weekend. Those two won't be bothering any of us again."

Corie released Matt's arm to exchange a hug with the dark-haired woman. "Thanks, Melissa."

"Thank your boyfriend here. By the way, my husband wants to meet you." Melissa smiled at Matt before nodding toward the booth beside her where Evan had spread out his toys, drawings and plastic building bricks. "Corie, take ten. I'll get your orders out for you."

Corie slid into the vinyl seat beside Evan while Matt pulled off his stocking cap and unzipped his coat. Although Corie spared a few moments to ruffle Evan's hair and inquire about the state of repairs on his dragon, when Matt settled onto the seat across from them, he felt her feet sliding between his under the table. He might have thought it was an accident until a few seconds later when her fingertips brushed against his knee. Although some surprisingly naughty thoughts leaped to mind at what they could be doing under the table, Matt chilled his brain and captured her hand in his, linking them together away from prying eyes.

"Sorry about the *boyfriend* thing," she apologized, capturing her bottom lip between her teeth in a frown. "Evan shouted it out to the restaurant as a warning to Harve and Jordy. I'm afraid the appellation stuck."

Man, how he wanted to kiss that bottom lip, ease her discomfort, ease his own. "I'm okay with that."

That sweet mouth blossomed into a smile. "I am, too."

Not for the first time, Matt noted how much he enjoyed holding this woman. How much he loved watching the nuances of her expression. How much he looked forward to hushed, intimate conversations like this one.

Sure, he'd spent part of the last few nights fantasizing about what it would be like to have Corie in his bed. As much as she seemed to like touching him, it wasn't a stretch to imagine undressing those decadent curves and tasting those soft lips and lying with her skin to skin, burying himself inside her, bringing them as close as two people could physically be. Although he knew her to be cautious, he also knew the woman who tugged him down for an impulsive kiss, who reached for him when he was being too careful for her, who stroked his lips and caressed his face and hugged herself around him in a way that was slightly possessive and made her smile that sexy, heart-robbing smile.

Yeah, even now, his body was aching to be closer to hers. But there was something just as soothing, just as satisfying about sharing a connection as simple as holding hands with Corie. With Evan babbling on with a play-by-play of how every brick fit together to rebuild his dragon, another waitress taking their order for coffees and cherry pie, his own thoughts racing as he tried to make sense of everything he was learning about the potential threat surrounding this family, holding hands with Corie under the table felt like a lot more. It was a secret bond for just the two of them to share.

It felt like something deeper, something stronger. Something permanent.

Matt was losing himself in the gentle green of Corie's eyes when his phone dinged with a text. Not wanting to release her hand, he set his phone on the tabletop and pulled up the message as soon as he saw it was from Cole.

Car registered to a Jeff Caldwell.
No record. Get this. His address is the same building as yours. You don't know him?

Matt frowned. He knew several of the people in his building. But he worked long hours. Kept to himself unless he had a family event. Or he was worried about Corie and Evan. The only Jeff he could think of was Wally Stinson's part-time super. And that was just a name to him. He'd never actually met the guy.

But he hated the idea that this guy had a link to Corie. What were the odds of another one of their neighbors showing up at the place where she worked? Of that same guy knowing Harve and Jordan? Of that man living in the apartment directly below hers?

"Ow."

For one fuzzy moment, Matt wondered at the change he saw in Corie's eyes. They were darker. Her pale brows were arched with a question.

Too late, he realized how much his grip had tightened and quickly released her hand. "Sorry."

"You didn't hurt me," she assured him. "But you went away somewhere. I'd say 'penny for your thoughts,' although I'm worried they're not good ones. Is this the spooky quiet side of you that you mentioned?"

His phone dinged with another text from Cole.

Without last names, it will take longer to ID Harve and Jordan. A buddy of mine, Sawyer Kincaid, just walked over from his desk and asked if I knew you. Said you got rid of the riffraff at his wife's restaurant. You're not thinking of switching sides and becoming a cop, are you? :)
I've attached Caldwell's license photo.
If you need anything else, let me know.
Stay safe.

He thanked his uncle and pulled up the photo. Although the man looked vaguely familiar, Matt couldn't place Jeff Caldwell as anyone he'd seen at their apartment building.

And though brown hair and brown eyes like his own were a fairly unremarkable look, he knew he'd seen this guy. But where? Matt splayed his thumb and forefinger across the screen, enlarging the picture to look for anything uniquely discernible, like a scar or crooked teeth. Beyond a spatter of brown freckles across his cheeks, he saw nothing to make this guy stand out in a crowd.

"Matt?" Now Corie's hands were both on top of the table, scooting aside their coffee mugs and reaching across to grasp his. "What's wrong? You're scaring me a little."

Right. This was the part where he usually lost the woman he was interested in—when he got locked up inside his head and failed to communicate.

But as he struggled to find the right words to say what was necessary without alarming her, Corie picked up his phone and flipped it over, hiding the screen. Her skin blanched as she sneaked a panicked glance at Evan. As soon as she saw her son was distracted, she leaned across the table, dropping her voice to a whisper. "Why do you have a picture of Kenny?" she whispered.

"Your ex?"

And just like that, all the niggling bits of information swimming through his brain made sense. It took every ounce of strength Matt possessed not to leap across the table and pull Corie and Evan into his arms.

He picked up his phone, turning the image away

from Evan and texting the information to his uncle. "His driver's license says Jeff Caldwell. This man is Kenny Norwell?"

"Yes. He's gained some weight and his hairline's receding a little, but that's him. Now answer *my* question. Why do you have that picture?" He followed the muscles contracting down her long, pale throat as she swallowed hard. "Spooky quiet isn't going to cut it tonight, Matt Taylor. I've worked hard to erase that man from my life. You need to talk to me."

Matt's gaze swiveled around the restaurant and landed on the reflections of the three of them in the window. He silently cursed that he couldn't see much beyond the glass besides traffic lights and streetlamps. How was he supposed to protect this family from a threat he couldn't see? "Have you seen him around any of the places you frequent? Here? Home? School?"

"No. Have you?"

He glanced across the table at Evan. "Maybe we shouldn't discuss this here."

She pulled her hands up inside the cuffs of her sweater and hugged her arms around her waist. Painfully aware of not wanting to alarm her son, Corie turned slightly in her seat. Although little more than a whisper, her tone was precise. "Ten words or less, Taylor. Tell me something before I get scared completely out of my mind."

He heard the sound of breaking glass in the distance and wondered if that was his hopes for a relationship with Corie crashing and burning.

"He owns the car Harve and Jordy drove off in."

For a moment, he thought she was going to pass out, there was so little color on her face. Matt reached clear across the table to cup her alarmingly cool cheek.

"Breathe, sweetheart. I'm not sure what's going on yet. But I will not let him hurt you."

Corie started to shake her head, her disbelief in his vow or his ability to make good on it evident in her hopeless expression. But then Evan suddenly rocketed to his feet, standing on the seat beside her, and her indomitable maternal instinct kicked in. "Whoa, sweetie. What are you doing?"

Ignoring her hands at his waist, Evan pressed his face to the glass, peering into the night. "Matt? Is that your truck?"

And then Matt realized he'd heard it, too. The breaking glass hadn't been in the restaurant or his imagination.

He spotted the flames shooting up from the windshield of his truck. Someone nearby was screaming. Others ran, both toward and away from the fire. He heard the squeal of tires spinning on the icy pavement, speeding in place until they found traction.

"Call 9-1-1." Matt grabbed his coat and rushed out the front door and into the street to deal with the blaze. "KCFD!" he shouted more than once, ordering pedestrians and vehicles out of harm's way as they slowed or stopped completely to watch the glowing liquid and the flames it carried with it spread across the hood and plop onto the pavement like a lava flow. He caught a glimpse of a white van racing away in the opposite direction as he vaulted into the back of his truck and pulled the fire extinguisher from the steel storage box there.

From his higher vantage point, he quickly assessed the potential hazards of the situation. The broken whiskey bottle and charred rag on the ground indicated someone had tossed an old-fashioned Molotov cocktail at his truck. Possibly the driver of the white van. Or Jeff Caldwell/Kenny Norwell or whatever he wanted to call himself. But he didn't see any dark muscle car racing away from the scene. Maybe Harve and Jordan had come back to exact revenge for the public humiliation of being bested in a one-sided fight.

And maybe he needed to be the firefighter he was and think about preventing personal injury or property damage. The vehicles were parked tightly together here. And traffic was becoming a slow bumper-to-bumper parade as concerts at bars or games on TV ended, and the patrons who'd been enjoying them left for home or their next entertainment destination. A lot of gas tanks in a confined space was a chain reaction fire waiting to happen. And if that flammable, tar-like substance got on anyone's clothes or skin, the slow-burning gelatin would be difficult to wash away, leaving horrible, painful wounds.

"Feel free to call 9-1-1," Matt yelled to the group of young twentysomethings circling closer, filming the fire. "Stay back!"

Traffic was backing up into the next intersection now, as drivers were too curious or frightened to pay attention to where they were going. If he didn't get control of this situation fast, he'd have a traffic accident to deal with, too.

Matt jumped down from the bed of his truck, shielded his face from the worst of the slowly expanding flames and laid down a layer of foam over his windshield and hood. While the driver parked in front of him thankfully arrived and moved his car out of harm's way, Matt continued to spray the extinguisher. But he was running out of juice fast because the viscous goop that was clearly the arsonist's weapon of choice was spreading faster than he could contain it.

Then he felt a hand at the small of his back. "Where should I spray this?"

What the hell? Matt whirled around on Corie. "Get back inside!" Instinctively, he circled an arm around her waist and walked her back toward the diner. Then he snatched her off her feet and spun her out of harm's way as a car swerved around them. She hadn't even stopped to put on a coat or gloves. "What are you doing here?"

She twisted out of his grasp and held up the small fire extinguisher she'd brought from the diner. "Enough atonement. You need help."

"You think this is about me needing to be a hero?" Her cheeks were chapped with the cold, and the only thing she had on over her polyester uniform was that navy-blue cardigan. "You'll freeze out here."

She completely ignored his arguments. "I called 9-1-1. They said they'd be here in a matter of minutes."

Shouts and honking from vehicles down the road who couldn't see what was happening this far up the road forced them to raise their voices. "What about Evan?"

"Melissa is with him. At least let me divert traffic."

"It's dangerous out here. And I'm not just talking about the fire."

"You can't face Kenny alone," she warned him, her gaze boldly searching his for understanding.

So, she thought her ex was responsible for this fire, too. She wasn't running or hiding. She was here to fight.

He shouldn't be turned on by that.

Matt tunneled his fingers into the silky hair at the base of her ponytail and dipped his head to capture her mouth in a quick kiss. Gratitude and understanding and something far more primal burned between them in the short seconds of that kiss. Then he peeled off his coat and draped it around her shoulders, taking the second extinguisher from her while she slid her arms into the sleeves.

"I'll handle traffic." He was tall enough to be seen over several vehicles down the road. He pointed to the flames dripping beside his front tire and pooling against the curb. "Lay down some foam along the edge of the sidewalk. We can't let this spread beyond my truck. Stay where I can see you. The guy who started this fire could still be part of this crowd somewhere. Evan needs you."

"And I need you." With a nod, Corie went to work. "Be careful."

She was soon joined by two men who'd brought fire extinguishers from one of the local businesses. Matt heard her repeating his orders, directing the other volunteers as he stepped into traffic and warned the next vehicle to slow down and give the burning truck a wide berth. He directed the oncoming cars into a single lane and urged the eastbound vehicles to cross the yellow line and keep moving.

As soon as he saw the B shift crew from Firehouse 13 turn the corner, Matt exhaled a sigh of relief. Once the police arrived and took over traffic duty, he jogged forward to meet the team and give them a sit-rep. One of them threw a bunker coat around his shoulders, identifying him as the firefighter he was. He shooed away the medic who wanted to check him for injuries and directed her to the civilian volunteers who'd helped them fight the fire. The threat to his truck had been neutralized, but he was more concerned about the puddles of incendiary goo still burning inside the perimeter Corie and the two volunteers had laid down before running out of suppressant foam. They'd need a hazmat unit to clean up whatever chemical had been inside the bottle. And they'd need to secure a sample to send to the crime lab to compare to the samples from the other fires.

As a police officer approached him to take his statement, Matt turned to watch Corie huddling inside his coat, watching his crewmates go to work. There was little more than that wheat-colored ponytail showing above the collar. Every cell in his body wanted to go to her, but he needed to make a full report before the perp or perps went to ground and couldn't be located until the next fire or something worse.

It was that *something worse* that was turning him inside out with a sense of impending doom. This fire had been personal. A message to him—the clock was ticking, Corie belonged to another man, he'd never be able to protect her. Or something as crudely prophetic as the fire that had destroyed Enrique Maldonado's car— stop talking to the cops...or die.

The problem with an arsonist working as an enforcer and sending graphic messages like this one was that there was a huge risk for collateral damage. Jobs stolen. People injured. Lives lost.

Matt wanted an APB out on Kenny Norwell, Harve and Jordy, and that muscle car, along with the white van.

He wanted Corie and Evan in his arms now. Brave, beautiful Corie who wasn't afraid of hard work or of him, and her brave, smart son who missed no detail and cared so much about others. Matt needed to know they were safe. He needed to see Corie's smile again. Every day of his life.

He needed to admit that he was long past falling in love with the family who lived across the hall. The family who needed him.

The family who made him need things that no bullying wiseacres, ex-hubby arsonist or killer was going to take from him.

Chapter Eleven

"I want to stop on the sixth floor." Corie had her keys out as she and Matt waited for the elevator. "Knock on that bastard's door and look him right in the eye."

Matt cradled Evan's sleeping weight against his chest. "It's after one in the morning, Corie. What if it isn't him?"

"Then I will apologize profusely and come upstairs to live the rest of my life in shame and paranoia."

He didn't even try to hide that hint of a grin that creased the chocolatey-cinnamon stubble of his late-night beard. But the grin vanished as suddenly as it had appeared by the time they stepped onto the elevator. "What if it is your ex-husband? Do you have a plan for what you'll say or do when you see him? Do you really want him to see Evan?"

"I'm sure he already has!" she snapped, then immediately dropped her voice back to a whisper. "Evan is the only thing he ever wanted from me. If he's stalking me and you, then he's seen Evan with one or both of us. If Jeff and Kenny really are the same person, I want to know it. He was in my apartment, Matt. He sabotaged my kitchen to start a fire. He could challenge me for custody of Evan if a judge heard about that."

"He's a felon with a criminal record. No one is going to take your son from you legally. You're too good a mother for that. And I won't let them do it any other way." He loosed one arm from around Evan to hug her to his side and dropped a quick kiss to her lips. "All right. I'll go knock on his door. You get Evan to bed."

"No. I'm coming with you. Either I'd be alone with Evan upstairs or I'd be alone down here. I don't want to be alone if Kenny has found us."

His shoulders lifted with a stalwart sigh. "I don't want that, either. But you'll take Evan, and I'll take point so he has to get through me first. If he's there, you take Ev and run. Call 9-1-1. Ask for Cole Taylor. Ask for any Taylor. Help will come."

"What will you be doing while we're running?"

"Having a conversation. Your ex ever have a penchant for guns or knives I should worry about?"

She shook her head. "But he knows how to set fires in a dozen different ways."

"I know how to put out fires in a dozen different ways."

No doubt. "He's strong, Matt. He knows how to fight."

Matt glanced down the straight line of his nose and over the jut of his broad shoulder at her. Right. Matt was strong and knew how to fight, too. He'd made short work of Harve and Jordy tonight. And though she knew Kenny would be more skilled and aware than either of those numb nuts had been, she had a feeling Matt could hold his own in any situation.

She leaned into him, hoping she wasn't asking too much of this good man. "I just want to live a normal life. Raise a healthy, happy son who isn't always worried about the monster coming and him losing me. I want friends and more children. I want to teach and love and live the life that Kenny and my mother cheated me out of. I don't want to be afraid anymore."

"Evan's a smart kid. Stronger than you think. You're stronger than you think. Besides, you've got that cool plastic dragon to protect you."

She giggled, patting the backpack that held Evan's creation, but her laugh was a wry sound that revealed more despair than humor. "You're our real protection dragon, Matt. You're big and strong and can harness the fire."

"I thought dragons were the bad guys until I met you two." His big yawn seemed to startle him. But Matt shook off his fatigue and stood up straighter, reaching across the elevator to push the number six button. "All right. We'll knock on our neighbor's door. If he was near the diner when we were and threw that Molotov cocktail, he won't be asleep, anyway."

A minute later, Corie was hefting her sleeping boy into her arms, along with his backpack and hers looped over either shoulder. Although he was slenderly built, Evan was a growing boy. She knew what a treat it was to have Matt literally shoulder some of the parenting burden from her. "I've got him," she assured him, reaching around Matt to knock on the door and start this meeting that was making the nerves roil in her stomach.

No answer.

Matt knocked. "Mr. Caldwell? It's Matt Taylor from the fire department." He put his ear to the door and knocked again, each time a little louder. "I don't think he's home."

A door opened across the hallway behind them and a woman in her pajamas and robe and a hot-pink scarf wrapped around her head peered through the gap between the door and jamb. "I know it's Friday night, folks. But do you know how late it is?"

Matt tipped the brim of the KCFD ball cap to her. "Yes, ma'am, I do."

She huffed at that answer and pulled her flowery robe more securely around her. "Well, some of us have to work on the weekend. Keep it down out here."

Corie stepped in when Matt's straight-to-the-point communication technique failed. She pointed to number 612. "Do you know Mr. Caldwell? Mr. Stinson's part-time super? I'm Corie McGuire, your neighbor from upstairs."

"Jeff keeps to himself. I like that about him." Not-so-subtle hint noted. The woman tipped her gaze up to Matt and frowned. Then she looked from Corie to her son dozing on her shoulder and frowned again. "He's up a little late, isn't he?"

Since they clearly weren't going to charm any information from this woman at this hour, Corie jumped on the first plausible lie that sprang to mind. "Yes, he is.

That's why we're looking for Jeff. I've locked myself out of our apartment. He has keys."

The woman dropped her gaze to the keys dangling from Corie's fingers before arching the sternest eyebrow she'd ever seen. "I'm calling Mr. Stinson. He'll deal with you."

The door closed on Corie's thank-you.

"You're a terrible liar," Matt teased, easing Evan from her arms until the building super arrived.

"Yeah. But I'm getting us into the apartment, aren't I?"

Well, technically, Wally Stinson was getting them into Jeff Caldwell's apartment.

Mr. Stinson looked less than thrilled when he stepped off the elevator in a pair of slacks and a wool robe hastily pulled on over his pajamas. His ring of master keys jingled as he shuffled along, smoothing his comb-over into some semblance of coverage on top of his head. "This isn't your place, Mrs. McGuire. Yours either, Mr. Taylor." He glanced over at the door to 613. "Miss Alice wasn't too happy that your noise in the hallway woke her up."

Corie didn't point out that his noisy key ring jangled more loudly than their knocking had. "It's vital that we speak to Mr. Caldwell. I think he broke into my apartment."

Wally frowned, debating whether or not her claim had any merit. "You said that before, that you think he jiggered with your oven."

"That's right."

"Any proof?"

Corie touched the door. "I think it's in here. I want to talk to him about it, but he isn't answering."

Mr. Stinson pushed his glasses up on the bridge of his nose. "That's because he works most nights at a distribution center. He only helps me during the day. Now y'all go on about your business and let the good people in this building get some sleep."

"That's even better." Corie darted in front of him to stop his retreat. "We could go in there without him knowing, see if any of my stuff is in there."

"I haven't gotten any complaints about other tenants being robbed." First this man had accused her son of setting fires, and now, like the woman in 613, he seemed to be calling her a liar. "Why would you think this man is stealing from you and messing with your things?"

She glanced over his head to Matt's steely expression. And when he nodded, Corie confessed what she suspected was true. "He's my ex-husband."

Wally's posture withered for a moment. "Ah, hell. I had no idea. We went through something like this with my daughter. Her no-account ex cleaned out every television and computer in the house when they were getting divorced. He pawned most of it." Wally gave her a pitying look and patted her shoulder as he changed direction and pulled out the key to unlock Jeff Caldwell's door. "If that's the case here, if he's taking or breaking your stuff, I'll fire him on the spot. But like I said, he usually isn't here nights."

"Then this is the perfect time to look, right? Thank you, Mr. Stinson."

Mr. Stinson opened the door to a dark apartment. He

turned on the light, and the place didn't look that much more welcoming, with a card table and chairs set up in the living room, and an old recliner facing a state-of-the-art television. There wasn't a single decoration or personal item anywhere.

Matt placed Evan back in her arms and led the way inside, his gaze constantly moving to take in every detail. "Doesn't look like he stays here much at all."

"Do you see what he took from you?" Mr. Stinson asked.

"What?" The super startled her from her inspection of a stack of porn magazines beside the recliner. He'd bought them retail. There was no subscription name or address on them. "There's hardly anything here."

"What did he take?"

Her sanity, peace of mind and well-being. But, of course, Mr. Stinson assumed a much more monetary reason for Kenny, er, Jeff, to be in her apartment. "Do you mind if we look around?"

"Your boyfriend already is."

Boyfriend. She really was getting used to having others link her and Matt together as a couple. She wondered if he minded.

She didn't. She didn't mind being linked to Matt Taylor at all.

"Corie." Matt's quiet tone filled her with more dread than a shouted warning would have. Hugging Evan tighter to her chest, she followed him to the kitchen. He put out his arm to keep her from moving any closer than the archway.

It didn't stop the sheer terror from reaching her,

though. The place was a science lab and an engineering station all rolled into one. There were stained measuring cups and hot plates on the counters. Jars filled with that clear, yellowish sludge that had coated the hood of Matt's truck and bubbled the paint up and melted his windshield wipers as it had burned. The same goo they'd found in the alley fire and inside her oven. There was an open toolbox with pliers and screwdrivers and a tinier metal box that looked like it was filled with delicate dental tools. On the floor was a box of wires and technical equipment—packaged disposable cell phones, computer chips, something that looked like bundles of firecrackers. On the opposite counter, there was a stash of three whiskey bottles whose labels matched the one that had shattered against Matt's truck. There were diagrams stuck to the refrigerator with magnets. There was a picture mounted there, too.

A well-worn, often-touched, picture of Evan when he'd turned one. They'd gone to the photography studio that day after Kenny had made her redress their son in a suit and Velcro tie instead of the cute baby blue overalls she'd put him in. There was a big *D* in the picture behind the posed shot—a *D* for Danny Norwell.

Even though he was sound asleep, she cupped the back of her son's head and turned him from the disturbing sight. The tears that stung her eyes were angry, fierce. This was her old life, the one she thought she'd escaped from. "This is Kenny. He used to have a setup like this in our garage back in St. Louis."

"Who's Kenny?" Mr. Stinson asked.

"Jeff, of course," she hastily corrected herself. "I guess he goes by Jeff now."

Matt had his cell phone out, snapping pictures. "I'm calling Uncle Cole. He and Agent Rand will definitely want to see this." He turned her toward the living room. "Stay here. I want to check out the rest of the place. Mr. Stinson, you'll stay here and watch her."

Although issued as an order, not a request, the older man nodded.

"We'll be fine," Corie assured him. "Just be careful."

Once Matt headed down the hall to the other rooms, Mr. Stinson pulled out one of the folding chairs for her, but she was too keyed up to relax. Not here. Not with evidence that pointed to the arson fires Matt had been forced to deal with. "Is this a meth lab?" the older man asked, nodding toward the kitchen.

"Something like." One thing Kenny had never whipped up in the garage was drugs. He'd always said he needed a clear head to work with the compounds he did create for clients who wanted a job done a certain way. "Some of those chemicals are combustible and flammable."

"What would he need those for?" Wally asked.

"Starting fires."

"Not in my building. He… I never knew any of this was here." Mr. Stinson ran his fingers through what was left of his thinning hair. "He knew his way around electricity, carpentry, plumbing—all of it. I played poker with him and a couple of his buddies one night."

"A couple of his buddies?" Corie almost sank in the chair as her knees wobbled beneath the weight of her suspicion. But she had Evan in her arms. She needed to be strong. Smart. Smarter than Kenny. "Does one of them have a dark, almost black beard? The other is tatted up. He's a redhead with freckles."

Wally nodded. "Yeah. Harve and—"

"Jordy."

He seemed surprised that she knew the men's names. Hell, she was surprised to know such things. Corie didn't know whether to be angry or feel foolish that she'd been in the dark about the danger creeping into the corners of her life for so long. "Do you know their last names?"

Wally scratched his head again, sorting through memories. "Jeff Caldwell, of course. Jordan Cox—we made a few jokes about his name. And Harve..." He snapped his fingers as the name fell into place. "Harve Mohrman. He told me he met Jeff in—"

"Jefferson City?" Prison. Harve and Jordy were prison buddies of Kenny's. Even Kenny's alias was a nod to his stay in the pen. Jeff Caldwell? Jeff City? Jeff C?

"Yeah. How did you know?"

Matt reappeared from the hallway, a dangerous purpose to his stride. "We need to go."

"Why? What did you see?"

He scooped Evan from her arms to hurry her along. "We may be disturbing a crime scene."

Something was wrong. Something was very wrong.

"What is it? A dead body?" Something worse than that? Something about her? Evan?

"Corie..."

She evaded his outstretched hand and hurried down the hallway, peeking into the first bedroom, the bathroom, ending up in the bedroom that was located where hers would be on the floor above them. As she entered the room, a sudden shock of cold seeped through her coat and clothes and chilled her skin.

But there was no window open. In the middle of January, there was no air-conditioning running.

It was the room itself, filled with hate and vengeance and the kind of obsession found only in horror and serial killer movies.

The smell got to her first. Something burned and pungent, like incense or a hundred scented candles. There was no furniture in the room besides a table and chair and a cardboard box that looked suspiciously like the one she'd set outside on her fire escape for the neighborhood cats.

Three of the four walls were a sick shrine to her. Pictures from her wedding to Kenny. Pictures from her childhood. Pictures of her waiting at the bus stop near Pearl's Diner, sitting on a bench on campus talking to a professor, monitoring recess duty at her school. There were pictures and newspaper clippings of fires, the shells of burned-out buildings, fiery car crashes and the charred remains of bodies. The images papered the walls and were decorated with bits of yarn pinned to the walls. Burned matches and broken lighters, even a perfume-size bottle of that flammable goo, hung from different strings. Spray painted over the collage of pictures were words and phrases like *child-stealer*, *kill the witch* and worse.

The fourth wall was tainted simply by being in the room with all the angry, vile images. It held pictures of Evan. Formal ones from when he was very young to candid shots of him on the playground at school here in Kansas City and one of him standing in the bed of Matt's truck, illuminated only by a streetlamp. If the kitchen had been the workspace of an arsonist, then this was his place of worship.

Corie couldn't move. She couldn't think, couldn't feel.

She could only startle when Matt walked into the room behind her, thankfully, having left Evan resting someplace where he couldn't see this. "Looks like he's been using the fire escape to go up to your apartment. That's possibly how he got in and out of your place."

It hadn't been a noisy alley cat pacing on her balcony. Kenny had been there, right outside her bedroom window, and she'd never even suspected.

There was so much hate, so much obsession in this room. She didn't know whether to scream or cry or simply surrender to the inevitable.

"Come on, sweetheart. Nobody needs to see this except the police." Matt turned her into his arms and walked her out of the room.

She leaned into him, grateful for his strength and support. "I never had a chance of living a normal life when I left Kenny, did I."

Chapter Twelve

Another two hours had passed by the time Detective Cole Taylor and NCIS agent Rand had finished their interviews and left Corie's apartment to go back down to apartment 612, where a team from the crime lab was processing the evidence in the elusive Jeff Caldwell's apartment and members of the KCFD were safely packaging and removing the flammable chemicals and fire-starting devices her ex-husband had kept there.

They were as certain Jeff Caldwell was Kenny Norwell as she was, although no one could find him. And they were certain he was the man a mobster named Chad Meade had hired to do some jobs for him, including torching a car and a building and covering up the scene of a murder. Cole Taylor and his NCIS partner had left discussing the possibility of Kenny turning state's evidence against Meade.

If they could capture him.

If he didn't find another way to hide himself in plain sight and never be found again.

Matt's uncle had also promised a round-the-clock watch on their building while his parents, brothers, sis-

ters-in-law and extended family members she'd lost
track of stopped by to bring food, offer a place to stay
and trade hugs, handshakes and promises of support that
extended to Corie and her son...because Matt said they
were important to him. Corie had never seen such an
outpouring of love before. Certainly, the Taylors were
nothing like life with her family or Kenny had been.
She'd met so many Taylors, she couldn't remember all
their names, much less put faces to which branch of
the family belonged with whom. But each and every
one of them had made her feel as welcome as Mark
and Amy had the other night. Like she was a part of
something bigger than herself. Part of that family she'd
always wanted. An extended family where she could
let her son visit a grandparent and know he would be
safe and nurtured and loved in a way Kenny and her
mother never could.

While the outpouring of love and support had gone
a long way to help her bury the images from Kenny's
kill the witch room, she had no doubt Kenny was tar-
geting her now, tormenting her for his own pleasure
or because he wanted her off her guard, giving him an
opportunity to steal back the son he'd accused her of
taking and punishing her for daring to want something
better, safer, more loving than the world that Kenny and
his crime buddies offered.

Somewhere along the way, Corie had gotten her second wind. Anything she could do to help the police
helped Evan, and she'd do anything for her son. She'd
brewed several pots of coffee and served up multiple
snacks brought by each of her guests. With all the com-

ings and goings, no matter how quiet they'd tried to be, Evan had awakened at two thirty. He'd eagerly talked to Pike Taylor, petted his K-9 partner, Hans, and arranged a tentative play date with Pike's son, Gideon. He'd carried his plastic dragon with him the entire time he'd joked with Mark and Amy and played host to their indulgent guests.

She would carry the fear, the sense of impending doom for them both. Seeing her son so happy tonight was worth anything she'd gone through in her life—and anything that was yet to come.

But now that all the Taylors were gone, save for one tall, overbuilt firefighter who she feared would give his life to protect her and Evan, she had a different problem on her hands.

Matt was exhausted. He'd hinted at having a rough day on the job, and she suspected that was the reason he'd been so late getting to the diner in the first place. As he hugged his mother and father and locked the door behind them, Matt leaned back against the door and exhaled a deep breath. He looked haggard and tired—always incredibly strong—but now suddenly vulnerable somehow. He'd done so much for her, so much for Evan. Maybe now he'd let her do something for him.

Corie crossed the room. She watched him breathe in deeply and open his eyes to give her one of those almost-there smiles before she reached up to gently cup his stubbled jaw. "You smell good," he murmured in a husky voice.

"And you look exhausted. Come with me." She linked her arm through his and walked him over to her sofa. "You've been this big presence hovering around the room all night, keeping watch. Now it's your turn to relax and regain some of your strength. Sit. I'm taking watch over this apartment tonight."

He folded his long legs and sat back against the cushions, although his dark, hungry gaze never left her. "Corie—"

"No." She placed a finger over his firm lips, silencing whatever protest he was about to make. "I don't remember which brother it was, but they promised that someone would be watching the building all night. I'm in charge inside these walls. You can drop your guard for a little while and rest."

"I *am* beat," he admitted, his lips brushing like a caress against her fingertip. "But I can't shake the feeling that there's something more I could be doing to stop this maniac and protect you."

"Atonement?" She nudged his knees apart and moved between them to sit on his lap. It put her in the rare position of being eye level with him, and she made the most of it by leaning forward to press a lingering kiss against his lips. His hands tightened on her thigh and hip as he sighed against her mouth and then deepened the kiss. Although his deliciously languid possession of her mouth kindled the good kind of fire deep inside her belly and made her breasts feel heavy with anticipation, she also suspected his leisurely response spoke to his fatigue. The man had a physical job. He'd had a physical night putting Harve and Jordy in their place and dealing with his truck. Then there was the emotional roller coaster of discovering Kenny's dangerous workspace and heinous obsession room. Plus, for a man who leaned to the introverted, quieter side of things, dealing with all the police and family and firefighters who'd been in the building these past two hours had probably taken a toll on him. She wondered if *exhaustion* was a strong enough word for what he was feeling right now.

And so, because this was about what Matt needed, and not the deliciously sinful and cherished way his mouth and hands made her feel, she broke off the kiss and tipped his head to gently press her lips to the shadows beneath each handsome eye. Then she hugged him close and whispered against his ear. "You don't owe me anything. You don't owe anyone another piece of your heart and soul and protection and dedication. You've repaid the price for that fire you set as a child a hundred times over. Set your crusade aside for a few minutes and let someone take care of you for a change."

His hands rubbed big circles up and down her back. "Corie, sweetheart, you don't have to do anything."

She pulled away, hating that he saw their relationship in such one-sided terms. Yes, he was incredibly strong and smart and just and wonderful, but he needed to understand that she intended to be an equal partner in this neighbors–turned–friends–turned something infinitely more precious that had grown between them. Kenny had kept her—like a trophy, like breeding stock. But he hadn't loved her, and he'd destroyed any effort to love him.

Matt Taylor was too good a man to feel like he still owed the world a debt. "I don't *have* to do anything. But I want to." She scooted off his lap and pushed him back into the cushions when he tried to stand with her. "Now. What do you need?" She didn't have a lot to offer, but she would grant him whatever he asked. "Something to eat? Drink? I've got cold milk or apple juice. Or I can make more coffee. Sorry, I don't have anything stronger. Do you need a quiet place to sleep for a while?"

He grabbed her hand, stopping her from going into the kitchen. His gaze raked over her from head to toe, stopping with particular interest on her mouth and breasts, telling her one thing he wanted. One thing she would willingly give him.

But then Evan dashed into the living room, reminding them both they weren't alone. "Are you going to bed, Matt?" Evan asked, jumping onto the sofa beside his favorite hero. "Mom said it's *way* past my bedtime. Is it past yours?"

"Yeah, bud. Your mom was just telling me that I need to get some shut-eye."

Evan looked crestfallen. "Oh. You're going back to your apartment now? You're leaving?"

Matt glanced up at Corie, and she answered the question he hadn't even asked. "He's staying with us tonight, sweetie."

"Yay!" Evan's cheer was cut off by a yawn that Matt quickly echoed.

Corie squeezed her son's shoulders. "Come on. Let's get you into bed so Matt can get the sleep he needs, too."

"Okay. 'Night, Matt." Evan fell forward across Matt's chest, winding his arms around his neck.

Matt's long arms gently completed the hug. "Good night."

Evan sat back, his eyes narrowed in an earnest frown. "Do you want my dragon to keep the bad things away for a while? I put his wings back on him and fixed his face."

Matt squeezed Evan to his chest again and brushed a kiss against his soft brown hair. "Nah. You keep him with you tonight. But thanks for havin' my back. Love you."

"Love you, too." And then Evan bounced off the couch and ran to his room, heedless of the two wide-eyed adults staring after him.

After the door to Evan's room closed, Matt glanced up to Corie. "Is that okay? He really does mean a lot to me. He…feels like family."

Corie smiled as the lingering warmth from Matt's kiss expanded to bathe her heart in sunshine. "I'm very okay with that. After all, if you're going to be in a relationship with me, you're going to be in a relationship with my son. And I can't think of a finer role model for him."

Although she sensed that he wanted to ask what she meant by *relationship*, Corie focused on the offer she'd made. "Close your eyes and rest, Matt. It'll take me ten minutes to get Evan back to sleep. Then I'll come back and slice you another piece of that pie if you want."

His dark lashes were already brushing his cheeks as she chastely kissed the top of his head and hurried after Evan. "Don't you worry about us—or anything else—for ten minutes. That's an order."

By the time Evan had dozed off and she'd changed into her pajamas and brushed her teeth, Matt was sound asleep on the couch. His long frame was spread out with his feet hanging off one end of the couch and his head angled up on the armrest at the other. His staunch expression that was more serious than handsome while he was awake had relaxed in slumber, easing the harsh line of his mouth. This rare glimpse of boyish abandon invited her to run her fingers across the crisp dark hair at his temple and press a kiss there.

She was glad she could do this little thing for him, giving him a quiet sanctuary free from worry and guilt, even if just for a few minutes. Because she was certain there was plenty to worry about in their future, judging by Kenny's vindictive behavior and the promise of his own personal retribution plastered across the bedroom walls below hers.

Even though this was a different apartment, and her door and windows here had been checked multiple times by Matt and at least three brothers and an uncle, the last place she wanted to go was her own room. Not alone, at any rate. Not by the fire escape window, where they suspected Kenny had lurked on at least one occasion. Corie feared that if she went into her bedroom and closed her eyes, all she would see were the vile, violent things on the walls right below hers.

Shaking off that unpleasant thought, she checked the front door to make sure it was secure. She needed sleep, too. Her bedroom might feel off-limits, but there was a cushy chair out here where she often fell asleep reading a book. After turning off the lamp, Corie retrieved a couple of throws from the hall closet. She came back to untie Matt's boots and tug them off as quietly as she could without waking him. Then she spread one of the throws over his sleeping body.

He'd earned his rest. He'd earned her gratitude and admiration. He'd earned her trust and compassion. She tucked a pillow beneath his head and kissed his grizzled cheek. Even though she smelled the soap from his shower, she still detected a whiff of the smoke from the fires he'd fought today and tonight. It felt so right, having him here. It was reassuring to know he was safe, too. For a little while, at least. She thought of him as the embodiment of security. But tonight, she would be the one to give him shelter. She would be what he needed tonight. Something tight and guarded unfurled in her chest as she gazed down at the man whose face was softened by the shadows.

She really had fallen for this good man.

Maybe she hadn't been as careful with the boots as she'd thought. Maybe this alert, wary man had simply sensed her presence. Or maybe she'd projected her wish into his head.

Before she turned away, Matt grabbed her hand and pulled her onto the couch with him. "I guess I needed a little more than ten minutes. Is this okay?" he asked, snaking his arm around her waist and pulling her back against his chest, spooning behind her. "I'll go back to my own apartment if you want."

"You're not going anywhere," she said as he pulled the blanket over them both. The heat of his body snugged so closely to hers quickly made her drowsy. This was bliss, to feel so important, so warm and wanted by a man. This was the dream she'd always had about finding the right man, and she drifted slowly, contentedly toward that dream.

But then Matt suddenly tensed behind her, his breath a sharp huff against the nape of her neck. "Dead bolt?"

Corie laughed and turned in his arms. "Already taken care of."

There wasn't much room to maneuver on the couch, but she ended up flat on her back, smiling up at his confused expression. "What did I say?"

"*Dead bolt.* I think it's becoming my code word that means you care. You say it to me every night when you leave."

He feathered his fingers through her loose hair, smiling down at her. "So, I don't have to come up with flowery words or recite any poetry to impress you?"

She grinned at the joke. "I don't think that's your style. It's not mine, either. I like honest and straightforward."

His eyes were dark, pools of midnight in the shadows above her. "I saw a man die in front of me tonight. Plunged to his death and there wasn't a damn thing I could do to save him." His fingers tightened briefly against her scalp and then he was rolling back against the cushions, his arm thrown over his eyes. Tears pricked her own eyes at the pain in his voice. "A little too honest and straightforward, hmm? Sorry about that."

Corie turned into him, hugging him tightly. "Oh, Matt, I'm so sorry. Why didn't you say anything?"

"I was a little preoccupied tonight."

"Taking care of my troubles when you had your

own." She pressed a kiss to the warm skin above his collar, stretched against him to tickle her lips against his stubbled neck and sup on the strong beat of his pulse there. "What do you need? How can I help?"

She nibbled on the point of his chin before batting his arm away from his face and crawling right on top of him to reach his mouth and offer him the gentle absolution of her kiss. Her legs parted and tangled with his, sliding between his muscular thighs, already discovering the responsive hardness behind the zipper of his jeans. The nap of her flannel bottoms caught against the denim and muscle underneath, creating pockets of vivid awareness where the material caught and pulled against her skin.

His lips chased after hers as she moved to explore the hard line of his jaw and the surprisingly supple spot beneath his ear that seemed to be packed with a bundle of nerves that made him gasp for breath. She rode the rise and fall of his chest as Matt sucked in several deep breaths to control his responses to her bold exploration. "I'm not good at explaining what I feel. What I need."

"Then show me."

At last, his arms settled around her again. He branded her butt with the palm of his hand and pulled her fully on top of him, dragging her most sensitive places against the hard friction of his body. Giving him the freedom to express himself without words seemed to unleash something powerful and hungry inside him.

With a ragged breath that sounded like her own needy moan, he palmed the back of her head and held her mouth against his, feasting on her lips, demanding she open for him before his tongue swept inside to claim hers. With her body draped over his like a blanket, they didn't need the throw she'd brought from the closet. They were already generating all the heat either of them could need. The throw quickly landed on the floor beside them, and the knit pajama top she wore followed right behind it.

Matt's hands were firebrands against her bare skin, urging her toward a euphoric release she'd never experienced before. She found the hem of his sweater and T-shirt and tugged them up his torso. Her hands were equally greedy as they slid inside to explore his strong, wide chest. She felt a quiver of muscle here, the tickle of crisp curls of hair there. The turgid male nub poking to attention beneath the stroke of her fingers.

Her world rocked in a dizzying circle as Matt suddenly sat up, spilling Corie into his lap. She helped him peel off his shirt and sweater, and then she slipped back in his arms, the heat of skin against skin making her feverish with desire. Making love with Kenny had never lasted this long, much less driven her into this frenzy of need, the eagerness to pleasure, this pure delight in being pleasured.

He lifted her slightly and dipped his head to pull the tip of her breast into his mouth. "Matt," she gasped, unfamiliar with the fiery arrows zinging from her sensitive nipples down to the weepy heaviness between her legs. "Is this…? Are we…?"

"I want you." She clawed her fingers into his hair, holding his wicked mouth against her straining breast as he worked the pebbled nipple between his tongue and lips and teeth and squeezed the other breast in his hand. "I want you," he repeated on a husky moan against her skin.

She had no problem understanding what he needed from her. Corie hoped she was being equally clear. "I'm yours."

To hell with atonement. This brave, good man needed healing, not penance. He needed to believe that whatever he'd done as a child did not make him the man he was today. He needed to know that he was perfect and loved. In her arms, he was most assuredly loved.

"Floor okay?" he breathed against her mouth before reclaiming her lips. "Need...more space."

Corie's answer was to lean back over the edge of the couch and pull Matt with her. They toppled onto the floor together, her landing eased by the rug and blanket and the support of Matt's arm. Then there was a fumble of hands, both eager and out of practice, as they shed the remainder of their clothes and pulled a condom from Matt's wallet. But every touch was a heady arousal, every bump was a perfect caress.

Then Matt was on top of her, sliding into her. Corie closed her eyes to savor her body's pure, primal response to his weight making the pressure building inside her almost unbearable. But he was holding himself back, balancing himself on his arms when she wanted to feel all of him against her.

Her eyes fluttered open and she caught him grimacing at the struggle being so patient with her was costing him. "Matt." She framed his face between her hands, ran them over his shoulders. She linked her heels around his hips. "Let go, Matt. Don't hold back. You're safe with me." She arched her body up into his. Her head fell back as he sank deeper inside her and began to move. As he took her to the peak and they crashed over together, Corie hugged him tight with her arms and her legs. "And I'm safe with you."

Sometime later, after redressing in a layer of clothes in case Evan should awaken early and find them together, Corie and Matt were spooning again on the couch, cocooned by the warmth of the blankets and each other's bodies. The weight of Matt's arm was a possessive band around her waist, but she didn't feel trapped. The tension that had consumed him earlier had eased, leaving her feeling cherished and necessary, not used the way sex with Kenny had been.

This was how it was supposed to be between a man and a woman.

Matt's body was a furnace at her back as he brushed her hair off her neck and whispered against her ear. "Dead bolt."

And as sleep rose to claim her, she smiled and closed her eyes. "I love you, too."

Smoke.

Matt blinked his eyes open to the darkness of early dawn, unsure if the haze in his vision was due to the hangover of sleep deprivation or if something more was going on here. When he had slept, he'd slept deeply, contentedly. But two hours wasn't nearly long enough. Corie's couch was half a foot too short for his long body, as the stiffness in his neck would attest to.

But Corie herself was a dream. The woman liked to snuggle in close as she slept in his arms, either teasing him with the pillowed mounds of her lush breasts flattened against his chest, or rubbing that sweet, round bottom against his groin. The weight of her in his arms had given him a subconscious sense of reassurance that she was safe—and an arousal that had led to a second, more leisurely, yet no less incendiary round of lovemaking following that cathartic, healing tumble onto the rug where she'd encouraged him to be his big, bad self with her and let his fears and guilt and haunting memories of a boy who had never been enough be consumed by their mutual passion.

He loved Corie McGuire. He hadn't said those exact words, but he'd felt them. He'd shown her.

Did she understand?

And then the reality of the moment slammed through him like shots from a gun and he sat up, wide-awake.

He was alone. Her apartment was filled with smoke.

His nose never lied. Where was the fire?

"Corie?" Matt tossed the blanket aside and stepped into his boots. He'd lace them up later. Right now, he needed to understand what was going on here, and he needed to find her. He grabbed his wrinkled sweater and slipped it on over his T-shirt and jeans. "Corie!"

"In here." A true mother, she'd run into Evan's room first and woken him. Rubbing the sleep from his eyes, the boy was groggy, hopefully from being unexpectedly roused from bed and not from smoke inhalation.

Matt knelt in front of him, checking for any signs of pulmonary distress. "Take a deep breath for me, bud."

No coughing fit. He squeezed Evan's shoulder as he stood, telling him everything would be all right. Then he reached over to cup the side of Corie's neck and jaw, sifting his fingers into the heavy silk of her hair. "You?"

"I'm fine." She pointed toward the kitchen. "Why didn't the smoke alarm go off?"

He wanted the answer to that question, too. But whys were for later. "Shoes, jeans on both of you now. We're evacuating until I know what's going on."

Corie steered Evan back into his room. "Winter coats?"

He nodded.

While they dressed, Matt called it in and made a quick tour of her apartment. In the kitchen he found that the smoke detector had no battery in it. It didn't take any stretch of the imagination to believe Kenny Norwell had entered the apartment again at some point to sabotage Corie's safety protocols. But if he was so hell-bent on getting his son back, why would he endanger Evan like this?

There was a bigger game being played here, and Matt worried he was already a step behind whatever Norwell had planned.

Protecting Corie and Evan was still job one. The police and his father's arson team could work on taking down Chad Meade and his firebug for hire—Matt's focus was much closer to home.

But he couldn't find an ignition point from any of the usual suspects—appliances, electrical outlets, improperly stored chemicals. The floor in Corie's bedroom felt spongy as he jogged across it to check the fire escape. Flames and smoke were pouring out of the window right below Corie's, blocking their descent. He didn't need a degree in fire science to understand what was happening.

He closed the door behind him and ran to the living room, gathering Corie and Evan and leading them straight to the door, where they all put on their coats. Corie looped her bag over her shoulder, and Evan had grabbed his most prized possession—his dragon.

"The apartment below yours is on fire," he said, helping Evan zip up that too-tight coat of his.

Corie pulled a stocking cap over Evan's head. "Mr. Caldwell's... Kenny set his own place on fire?"

Matt checked the door to make sure it was safe to open, then ushered them both into the hallway. The smoke wasn't as thick here, but the haze hanging in the air told him it was seeping upward through every available vent, crack or open window. The flames would follow soon enough.

"We need to evacuate this floor and everything above us."

Corie nodded and jogged to the fire alarm on the wall. But when she pulled it, nothing happened. "This isn't working, either."

Matt ran to the far end of the hall and tried that alarm. Silence. Corie's ex had been very thorough.

He pounded on each door he passed, "Fire! KCFD, you need to evacuate. Fire!" A few doors opened immediately, and Matt repeated his orders. "Make sure your neighbors get out."

He rejoined Corie and Evan and guided them toward the stairwell, doing his best to ignore the twin sets of green eyes that were so wide with fear. "You need to get out of here, too. Stay off the elevator. Take the emergency stairs."

Corie grabbed a fistful of his coat. "What about you?"

"I'm a firefighter, sweetheart. I need to do my job. And I need to know you two are safe so I can do that job right."

Her grip tightened on his coat and she pulled him down to exchange a quick, hard kiss. "Do it well. We need you."

He walked them down to the sixth-floor landing, intending to part ways. He wanted to check out Norwell's apartment and get the other residents on the floor evacuated.

But a determined eight-year-old blocked his path. "I want to stay with you." Evan hugged his dinosaur in his arms. "I'm not afraid."

Matt went down on one knee in front of Evan and hunkered lower to look him in the eye. "You're the bravest boy I know, bud. But you need to respect the fire. Get your mom outside and the two of you stay together until I can reach you. Can you do that for me?" A familiar inspiration hit him, and he unbuckled his watch and strapped it onto Evan's wrist. "Here. Set the timer for ten minutes. I'll be down to join you by then."

"Ten minutes? Dragon swear?"

Matt crossed his heart. "Now go."

Hand in protective hand, the two most cherished people in the world to him walked away. Matt hurried onto the sixth floor, relieved to hear the blare of sirens in the distance. He knocked on doors and scooted the startled residents out to the emergency exits. He stopped when he reached the bowed door of apartment 612. The crime scene tape crisscrossing the door had been sliced through. He heard the rumble of something on the other side, like the whooshing ebb and flow of the tide rising along the beach. He knew that sound—heat, pressure, flames filling the confined space. This whole area was about to blow.

The snooty lady across hall was only too happy to have him knocking on doors now. As he turned her to follow her neighbors to the exit stairs, Matt tried to reason out why Norwell would torch his own apartment. KCPD and the crime lab had already been in there to gather evidence against him. The fire endangered his son. An explosion could destabilize the building's structure, bringing it down on all of them, killing anyone who couldn't get out.

The evacuation.

Matt swore. This was all about getting Evan and Corie out in the open. It was about hiding in a crowd distracted by noise and fear.

It was about kidnapping his son. Again.

Matt pulled out his phone to call Corie to warn her.

And that's when he heard the man screaming for help.

From apartment 612.

"Help me! Somebody, help!"

Matt's heart sank. He had no choice. People before property. And he wasn't going to have another Enrique

Maldonado flinging himself off a balcony because he couldn't escape the flames and smoke.

Matt texted his brother Mark, told him his location and what he was about to do. Then he steeled himself with a deep breath, prepared himself for the blast of heat, and kicked in the door. Fire literally poured out into the hallway as the man's screams turned to gratitude. "Hey, it's the boyfriend. Help me. Please."

In between hacking coughs, he recognized the man's voice. Jordan Cox. For half a second, Matt thought about turning around and running downstairs to Corie instead of rescuing this worthless piece of trash. But he'd already notified his team that he was going in, and they'd risk their lives looking for *him* if he didn't show up where he said he'd be.

He hoped his boots were thick enough to protect him from this walk through hell. "Shut up and do what I tell you this time," he commanded, racing into the searing heat and toxic fumes. "You take in more smoke if you talk."

The damn fool wouldn't listen. While Matt pulled out his pocketknife and cut Jordy free of the duct tape he'd been bound with, the redheaded bully prattled on. "He said he didn't need my help anymore, that I was a liability. He said he could kill two birds with one stone. Please don't let me die."

Despite a blow to the head, probably to subdue him long enough to bind him to the chair, Jordan seemed aware and ambulatory. Still, he'd never make it through this fiery sludge in those tennis shoes. Since time was of the essence, there was no debate. Matt put his shoulder to Jordy's midsection, secured his arms and legs and lifted him up in a fireman's carry.

With flames melting the carpet and igniting the wood subfloor in the hallway now, Matt carried the smaller man to the exit stairs. There he set him down, but clamped a hand around Jordy's arm, partly to keep the man standing and moving through every cough, and partly because he intended to hand him over to the first police officer they met once they got outside.

On the third floor, he asked, "Did Norwell hire you to harass Corie?"

"Yes, sir."

"Why?"

"'Cause he's pissed at her for taking his son. He wanted us to rough her up, scare her a little. He said he was too busy to do all the work himself." On the second floor, Jordy tried to apologize. "He doesn't like that you're in the picture. He said he had to change his plans once you got involved."

"Do you know his plans now?"

Jordy shied away, knowing Matt wouldn't like his answer. "Keep the kid. Kill your girlfriend."

"Move."

The air was cold when they made it outside, but it was also clean. Matt sucked two deep breaths of reviving air into his lungs. Most of the cops out here were managing traffic and crowd control, but he got rid of Jordy and started his search to find the McGuires.

He found the building super first. "Stinson! You got a list of tenants we can go through to confirm that everyone has evacuated?"

The older man pulled it up on his phone and started checking people off.

Where was the woman with hair the color of a ripe wheat field and whose smile lit up his heart? And that spunky little boy who was everything Matt could want in a child of his own?

He skimmed the crowd again, his training not allowing the man in him to panic. He even glanced at the passersby pausing their morning walks and commutes to work to ogle the drama of lights and fire engines and flames and dark smoke pouring out the sixth-floor window. They should have made it down and out through the exit stairs ahead of him. The tension in his neck corded up with the very worst of warnings and he ran back to Stinson. "Where are Corie and Evan?"

"They aren't with you?"

"I sent them down ten minutes ago."

The balding man scrolled through the list on his phone. There were no checks beside the tenants of apartment 712. "I haven't seen them."

When he spotted a familiar white van parked against the curb halfway down the block, Matt ran to it. "Corie! Ev!"

Inside, he found a remote arson lab with nearly all the same ingredients and equipment Norwell had kept in his apartment. He also found Harve Mohrman unconscious and bleeding from a head wound. Was he supposed to suffer the same fate as his buddy Jordy? Had Norwell's attempt to kidnap Evan from the crowd outside their burning building failed? If so, where were Corie and Evan now? Or was leaving the van unlocked and in the open like this an impromptu attempt to frame Mr. Gross Beard for all the arson fires?

Matt stepped out of the van and made three calls, summoning a medic to treat Mohrman, a cop to arrest him, and Corie's cell.

It went straight to voice mail. Again.

And then he saw the black muscle car, already three blocks down, darting through the growing crowd of rush-hour traffic, speeding away. The damn van was one more misdirection giving Norwell more time to get away with his prize.

Not this time. Matt wasn't sure what to do next. He couldn't afford getting caught by another diversion. He'd lose all trace of Norwell before he got down to his truck in the parking garage. If Norwell had Corie, she was as good as dead. If he had Evan, the boy was as good as gone.

No. No way. He'd lost one family in a fire. He wouldn't lose another.

He spotted Kyle Redding's white scene commander helmet and ran. "Captain!" Then he saw the engine parked farthest from the scene and changed direction. When he saw the Lucky 13 logo on the side, he kissed it with his hand and climbed inside behind the wheel. He hadn't understood all of the changes that had happened in his life this past week, but he knew one thing very, very well.

He turned the key over in the ignition, and the engine's powerful motor roared to life.

But Redding had chased after him, grabbing the door before Matt could close it. "Taylor! What are you doing with my engine? You're supposed to be off the clock today."

"Take it out of my paycheck, boss." The car was still in sight but getting farther away. If it turned a corner or crested a hill… "Ignition point is apartment 612. Flames are in the hallway encroaching on the apartment above it." Corie's apartment. "I've got a secondary emergency, sir. Let me go."

His brother Mark was there, too, opening the passenger side and climbing in. "Come on, bro. Talk to us. What's wrong?"

"He took them."

"Corie's ex? He took the kid, too?"

Matt turned on the lights and siren. He'd clear a path through traffic and get to them quicker this way. "Call Cole and Rand. Tell them I've got a bead on Norwell. Give them the GPS on my engine and follow me."

"I'll handle the tracking," Redding insisted, climbing down and calling dispatch. "You're on my orders, Taylor," Redding said, giving Matt the backup he needed to keep his job. Stealing a fire engine for a personal mission tended to get one fired. And jailed. "Go find this guy who's burning up my city and give him hell."

"Captain?"

"I had a woman I loved once, too." He tapped the door of the truck, signaling Matt he was clear to move out before striding away. "Go! I want that arsonist behind bars."

Instead of jumping down, Mark put a helmet on Matt's head and tossed a coat around his shoulders. "You don't have to do this, Mark."

His baby brother grinned. "Hell yeah, I do. We're a team, remember? We have been since the day I was born." He smacked Matt's shoulder the same way Captain Redding had tapped the truck. "Lucky 13 rolling."

Chapter Thirteen

Corie woke up to throbbing headache and the coppery taste of blood in her mouth.

A pungent chemical smell hung in the air, stinging her sinuses, and making her eyes water. But when she reached up to wipe the tears from her cheeks, a sharp pain tore at her wrists, pulling out some of the hair and bruising her skin. What the…?

Crystal clarity returned with a vengeance and she sat up straight. She was strapped to a rolling office chair, her wrists and ankles bound by duct tape. That same yellowish goo Matt had showed her from her oven fire had been painted in a large circle around her chair. Her clothes were damp with it, too.

Now she remembered the figure she'd seen in the smoke when she and Evan had been evacuating their apartment building. She'd assumed it was another resident following them down the stairs. But then he'd run up on her.

She'd known one frightening moment of recognition as the man's face cleared the smoke. Dark hair. Thick chest. Cold eyes. She'd instinctively pushed Evan behind her as Kenny's fist connected with her cheek, split-ting it open and emptying out a bucket of ball bearings that swirled inside her skull. She fell to her knees as Evan screamed and reached out for her.

But Kenny got between them first, cupping his hand beneath the boy's chin. "Remember me, son?"

Evan backed into the corner of the stairwell landing, avoiding his father's touch. Since sentimentality hadn't worked to instantly win him over, Kenny went back to the tactics he knew best. He jerked Corie to her feet, the sudden movement doing nothing to help the con-cussion he'd probably given her. "Kenny, don't do this," she pleaded as the world spun in circles around her. "He doesn't know you. All you're doing is scaring him."

"Good. Then he'll understand." Kenny's grip tight-ened painfully on her arm, keeping her upright when she would have stumbled. "You do exactly as I say, Danny, or I will hit her again. Now come with me. And act like we're all just going for a nice little stroll."

Corie had barely made it to his fancy black car when the dizziness made her puke. She'd passed out in the back seat without knowing if her son was safe. Now, minutes? Hours? Sometime later, the very chemical that was supposed to kill her had acted like smelling salts and roused her to awareness.

She quickly took in her surroundings. Judging by the large louvered windows running the length of the walls, it looked like she was on an upper floor of a con-verted warehouse. She seemed to be smack-dab in the center in an open commons area. But on either side of her were cubicle walls, desks, papers. It was Saturday and these offices were closed. So, there were no employees she could call on for help.

She spotted Evan at one of the windows, kneeling on a stack of office chairs and looking out at something through the window that had been propped open. Under normal circumstances, she'd have been frightened to see him leaning so close to an open second-story window. But these circumstances were far from normal, and right now she was helpless to keep either of them safe. At least he had his dragon with him to give himself comfort. He hugged it to his chest and rocked back and forth.

Corie frowned as her vision cleared. No. He was picking the dragon apart, piece by piece, glancing over his shoulder to the cubicles on her right and then dropping the colorful plastic bricks one or two at a time out the window.

They both turned their heads to the sound of raised voices as two men argued behind one of the dividing cubicle walls.

"I said no moonlighting."

"I've done every job you've hired me to. The results have been satisfactory, yes?" She recognized Kenny's voice immediately.

"Yes. But I'm not paying you to screw with your ex-wife. You're drawing too much attention to my operation."

"You said you wanted this building burned to the ground. You don't get to say how I do it."

"I pay you good money to take care of my enemies."

"And I will. These boys will be in bankruptcy long

before they think of horning in on your territory again.
This job takes care of two problems—yours and mine."
Corie heard footsteps and knew the men were on the
move. "Now give it a rest, Meade."

Corie sat up as straight as her bindings allowed, trying to get a glimpse of whom Kenny was arguing with.
Maybe she could convince that man to help her. Maybe
he'd at least take Evan with him and drop him off at
police station or firehouse. Maybe she had a chance to
at least keep her son safe.

Her movement caught Evan's attention, and he saw
that she was awake. "Mom!"

He jumped down from the stack of chairs and ran
toward her.

"Evan, stop!" She eyed the puddle of goopy gel and
knew Kenny had rigged this whole place to go up in
flames along with her. "Stay back! Don't get any of this
stuff on you. It'll burn, sweetie."

A hard arm in steel-gray coveralls caught Evan by
the shoulder and pulled him several feet away from the
flammable gel. "Your mom's right, Danny."

"I'm not Danny!" Her boy twisted away and kicked
Kenny square in the shin. "The dragon beats the monster every time!"

"What does that even mean?" Kenny was still rubbing his injured leg and cursing. "What kind of garbage
you teaching my son, Katie?" He turned his curses on
Evan and Corie nearly ripped her arms from their sock-
ets trying to break free and get to him to protect him.
"You need to man up, kid. No son of mine is going to
believe in all this pansy fairy-tale stuff." He snatched

the dragon from Evan's hands. "What is this supposed to be, anyway?" He tossed the dragon at Corie. She ducked, but the toy hit the floor hard and broke into several pieces.

"No!" Evan shouted, lunging after his longtime version of a security blanket.

"Evan, stop!" she shouted, not wanting him any closer to this death trap. "Do as he says. Please."

"Stop calling him Evan. His name is Danny, after my dad."

Evan swung his small fists at the monster who'd sired him. "It is not! Matt's my dad now. He's Mom's boyfriend and he loves me. Matt said so."

Kenny backhanded him across the mouth. "Shut up—"

Corie came unglued, sliding forward in her chair and crashing to the floor. "Don't you touch him! Evan!"

"There ain't no other man who's your daddy but me."

The man Kenny had addressed as Meade stepped out from behind the cubicle wall. He had graying hair, and though he wore a pricey tailored wool dress coat over his suit, she could tell he wasn't a classy guy. He walked right past Evan, who sat on the floor, holding his cheek and sobbing. He didn't offer a handkerchief or a smile or ask if Ev was okay. That man was no ally to her. "I'm leaving. I was never here. I've had my fill of domestic squabbles years ago. You're fired."

"I've got what I want," Kenny shot back, clearly uncowed by the man's intended threat. "I've got plenty of money in my bank account and I've got my boy."

The older man turned and pointed a finger at Kenny. "If I hear that you've stayed in the country…"

"You'll hire another enforcer to come after me?" Kenny laughed. "Let 'em try. I have a reputation as the best in the business for a reason. Your secrets are safe with me, Meade." He waved off the man who had employed him. "Now get out of here and let me work."

Kenny picked up a bag she assumed was full of tools or money or both and started packing the items he'd used to imprison her and prep the building for the fire. But he had no pity for her son, either.

Corie managed to push herself up onto one elbow, putting her at Evan's level. "Hey, son. Look at me." Her poor baby had a mark on his face, and his eyes were puffy and red. But he was her brave little soldier. He sniffed hard and swiped away his tears. That's when the saw the black watch that was far too big for him dangling from his wrist. She wasn't giving up hope until her very last breath. She wasn't letting her son give up, either. "Look at your watch and practice telling time. Start counting how many minutes it takes for Matt to get here."

Kenny laughed at what he thought was a ridiculous challenge. "Your boyfriend isn't coming to save you, Katie. I left him with plenty to do. He'll never find you. Not until this place has burned to the ground and Danny and I are on a plane to a tropical beach in the Caribbean."

Corie didn't intimidate the way she used to. She wasn't isolated and vulnerable to the likes of Kenny

Norwell or her mother anymore. She had friends. She had the makings of a new family. She had a future.

She had her very own fire-eating dragon.

"You don't know Matt Taylor."

MATT DROVE THE fire engine up and down the skinny throughways and parking areas in the warehouse district north of City Market. He'd killed the lights and siren, creating as much stealth as a diesel truck this size could manage. He'd wasted too many minutes getting stuck behind a line of vehicles merging into one lane around a construction site. If he'd been thinking, he'd have had dispatch clear a construction-free route for him.

But he hadn't been thinking. He'd only been feeling. Fear. Love. Loss. Anger. He needed Corie to get inside his head and help him make sense of it all. He needed her beautiful smile to keep the shadows of the past at bay. He needed her boy to make him laugh and get him excited about being a father. He needed her. Period.

Mark's sharp eyes had kept the black Charger in sight until it had turned off into this maze of old manufacturing plants and shipping warehouses that had been converted into office buildings, condos and modern businesses.

"Where's the car, Mark? Where did he take them?"

Ironically, Mark, the comic of the family, was the one who kept a cool head. "It's only been a couple of minutes since we lost them. He probably drove into one of these warehouses and pulled down the door to hide. He's still here. This complex is locked down for the weekend. We'd have heard him driving away."

Matt glanced across the cab of the truck, wanting to believe. But searching every warehouse, garage door, even just on this single block was a daunting task. "We need backup. Call it in. Call everybody in. Alex. Pike. Mom and Dad."

Mark pulled out his cell phone and picked up the radio off the dashboard. "I'll get on the horn with them and any personnel from the nearest station who can give us a hand."

"I can't lose them, Mark. It's the first time it's ever felt right for me. I can talk to her and…she says I'm funny and…"

Matt's gaze zeroed in on the small dots of primary colors and purple and green sprinkled across the pavement in front of the shipping door off to his left. "Hold on."

While Mark chatted with dispatch, Matt climbed down from the truck to figure out what he was looking at. His mood lightened with every step. He picked one, and then another, cradling the tiny plastic building blocks in hand. He glanced up at the second-story window that had been propped open and knew these were a deliberate clue. "Evan McGuire, if you're not careful, I'm going to adopt you."

Tucking the bricks into his pocket, Matt searched for a ladder or fire escape that would give him the access he needed to see inside the warehouse. A dumpster and the drainpipe above it did the trick, too. Although Matt couldn't see into the open window from his vantage point, he could see in.

He nearly lost his grip and plummeted to the ground

at the sight of Corie strapped to a chair and lying in a puddle of Kenny Norwell's home-brewed fire-starter kit. The setup was just like the fire that killed Enrique Maldonado.

After a quick descent, he climbed back into the fire engine and shifted it into gear. "That place is rigged to burn and Corie's trapped in the middle of it. She won't be able to get herself out."

"Backup's en route. Did you get eyes on Evan?"

"No. But Norwell's there, so the kid has to be around someplace." He knew a lot of different ways to prevent fires, to put out fires, to rescue someone trapped in a fire. But a locked door stood between him and getting the job done. "We get one shot at this, Mark. Once Norwell knows we're onto him, Corie will be at his mercy."

"You know I'll follow your lead. What do we do?"

And then he knew. A moment of clarity washed over Matt like one of Corie's smiles. He shifted the engine into reverse, backed into an alley, then straightened the big machine to meet the shipping bay door at a ninety-degree angle. "Hold on to something."

"You're not gonna…?" Mark buckled himself in and grabbed the hand bars as Matt shifted gears and stomped on the gas. "Whoa, baby! Who said you were the shy one?"

MEADE AND KENNY were arguing again.

Kenny never had played well with others. "When we made the agreement to work together on the outside, I said yes because the money is good. But I am my own boss. Understand?"

On the outside? Kenny and this Meade had been in prison together?

She wasn't sure how that was helpful, other than with the two roosters going at each other, each trying to assert his superiority over the other, they weren't paying any attention to her. Kenny probably believed he'd put her in an inescapable trap, and Meade didn't care.

Since she was already covered in the accelerant, it didn't make any difference if she got more on her. So Corie was tapping every last bit of her strength to crawl her way to one of the desks. She wasn't sure how she was going to lever herself up high enough, but one of those drawers or pencil caddies had to have a pair of scissors or a box cutter she could use to free herself.

Evan was back on his stack of chairs beneath the windows, thankfully engrossed in watching the dials on Matt's watch and, without realizing it, believing in a miracle.

Corie had her teeth hooked onto the edge of a drawer and, millimeter by millimeter was tugging it open when she heard the loud roar of an engine outside. Both men turn to look toward the window. "What the hell is that?"

The entire building shook, and Corie fell to the floor as something big and powerful crashed through the garage door below them.

Evan tumbled off his perch but quickly climbed back up to peer out the window. "It's Matt! It's his fire engine!" He swung around to share the news with Corie. "He's here!"

"Evan, run!" He hesitated for a moment, no doubt concerned for her. "Run!"

He took off, leaving her sight as he raced for the far door as fast as his little legs could take him. She heard voices shouting down below, running footsteps, someone calling her name. There were sirens outside now, too. She could barely hear herself think.

But Corie could see the look of pure hatred on Kenny's face.

"You'll never take my son from me again." He flicked a match between his thumb and finger and dropped it into the puddle of chemicals that covered the floor. The goo burst into flame like a burning pool of oil and raced across the room toward her. "Die, witch."

He took off after Evan. "No!"

The next several things happened so quickly that Corie wondered if her concussed brain was hallucinating.

The nearer door burst open and two firefighters rushed in with a hose.

"Corie!"

Matt? "I'm over here."

Two police officers rushed in behind them, guns drawn. A rangy German shepherd led another officer inside ahead of a shorter man armed with some kind of assault rifle. Matt used hand signals to send them all off in different directions. "The boy is our number one priority."

He left the other firefighter to open up the nozzle and spray a gushing waterfall that wiped Mr. Meade off his feet. Then he turned the hose, catching the edge of the fire trap with a powerful stream of water.

"That's all the length we've got, Matt!" Mark Taylor. "I can't reach her."

"I can."

Matt ran straight toward her, his thick boots and bunker gear the only deterrent he needed to race through the flames and kneel beside her. "Matt! Don't!"

He pulled a knife from deep inside his coat and flipped it open to slice away the tape that bound her right wrist. He trailed a gloved finger over her bruised, swollen cheek. "Oh God, sweetheart, you're hurt."

"Should I tell you I've had worse?"

"No." He moved to her right leg.

Even though she couldn't feel her fingers, she still reached to rest her hand against his stubbled cheek. "I love you."

"I love you." He looked up from freeing her left wrist. "Wow. That was easy to say."

"You're a strange one, Matt Taylor. But I think you're the right one for me."

"Yeah?"

"Yeah. That's why you have to go. This isn't safe. I need someone who loves Evan to be with him now."

"*You* love him. *You'll* be with him." He never glanced over his shoulder while he cut the last of her restraints. But Corie had a clear, eye-level view of the fire dancing across the pool of accelerant, following the path that led straight to her. "You have to go. I'm about to go up in flames."

"Then it's a good thing I'm a firefighter." He shrugged out of his bunker coat and wrapped her inside it. Corie felt rather than saw the heat of the flames reach for her as he carried her through the fire. Seconds later, he set her on her feet and tossed the coat aside. They were near the windows now, several yards beyond the perimeter of the fire. "Get these clothes off."

She fumbled with the buttons on her sweater and blouse while he unsnapped her jeans and peeled them down her legs. "You have to go after Evan. He went out the other way."

"He's got a lot of people I trust looking out for him."

"But—"

"You've raised a smart kid. His trail of breadcrumbs is how I found you." He tossed the last piece of tape aside. "Clothes, woman. I don't want any accidental spark to trigger a reaction. I don't intend to lose you."

"My hands are numb. The circulation's been cut off."

"Understood." He took over and stripped her down to her bra and panties and gathered her into his arms. For a split second, she looked up into warm brown eyes and knew she would be safe. She knew she could trust his word that her son would be safe, too. "Hold your breath. This is going to hurt."

Corie filled her lungs with air and buried her face against Matt's chest. He clutched her tightly against him as Mark hit them with the full blast of the fire hose. By the time Matt signaled his brother to cut off the hose, several other firefighters were streaming in with longer hoses that allowed them to reach the spread of the chemicals and douse the flames.

She felt Matt's lips at the crown of her hair. "I don't smell it on you anymore. I think it's safe to move you outside now. I want you checked out by a medic."

She felt like she'd been hit by a freight train, and she was already starting to shiver after being drenched to the skin. But there was still only one thing on her mind. "I'm not doing anything else until I see my son."

"How about you put on some dry, chemical-free clothes? Blanket!" Matt gave the order, and seconds later Corie had two blankets, one wrapped around her like a sarong, and the other draped over her shoulders. "Evan's okay, sweetheart. He's with my mom and dad in an ambulance, getting checked over by medics. Norwell and Meade have been arrested by my uncle Cole. Jordy turned himself in, and Harve is on his way to the hospital. I'm guessing he's got jail time in his future, too."

Corie stared up at Matt, dumbfounded. "How? How do you know all that? How can you be so certain?"

He pulled the earbud out of his ear and showed her that he'd been listening in to official radio chatter this entire time. "A little birdie told me."

Corie didn't know if she wanted to swat him or hug him. "Why didn't you tell me?"

He smoothed her wet hair away from the wound on her cheek and tucked it behind her ear. "You were the one in imminent danger. That's where my focus needed to be."

"Atonement?"

"No. Love." Then he gently laced his fingers together with hers. "Let's go get our boy."

* * * * *

Don't miss the previous book in USA TODAY
*bestselling author Julie Miller's The Taylor Clan:
Firehouse 13 series:*

Crime Scene Cover-Up

*Available now wherever Harlequin Intrigue
books are sold!*

COMING NEXT MONTH FROM

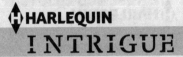

Available January 26, 2021

#1977 HUNTING A KILLER
Tactical Crime Division: Traverse City • by Nicole Helm
When K-9 handler Serena Lopez discovers her half brother's a fugitive from justice, she must find him—and his dangerous crew. It's a good thing her partner is lead agent Axel Morrow. But as cunning as the duo may be, it's a race against time to catch the criminals before they kill again.

#1978 PURSUIT OF THE TRUTH
West Investigations • by K.D. Richards
Security expert Ryan West's worst fears come to life when hotel CEO Nadia Shelton is nearly killed. Someone will do anything to find the brother Nadia thought was dead, and Ryan will have to stay strictly professional to protect her. But the sparks igniting between them are impossible to ignore.

#1979 HIDEOUT AT WHISKEY GULCH
The Outriders Series • by Elle James
After saving a woman and baby from would-be kidnappers, ex-marine Matt Hennessey must help Aubrey Blanchard search for the baby's abducted sister. Can they bring down a human trafficking cartel in the process?

#1980 THE WITNESS
A Marshal Law Novel • by Nichole Severn
Checking in on his witness in protective custody, marshal Finn Reed finds Camille Goodman fighting an attacker. Finn is determined to keep the strong-willed redhead alive, but soon a serial killer's twisted game is playing out—one that the deputy and his fearless witness may not survive.

#1981 A LOADED QUESTION
STEALTH: Shadow Team • by Danica Winters
When a sniper shoots at STEALTH contractor Troy Spade, he knows he must cooperate with the FBI. As Troy and Agent Kate Scot get closer to the truth, secrets from Kate's family will be revealed. How are they involved...and what are they willing to do to keep themselves safe?

#1982 COLD CASE COLORADO
An Unsolved Mystery Book • by Cassie Miles
Vanessa Whitman moves into her eccentric uncle's remote castle to ghostwrite his memoir, but then Sheriff Ty Coleman discovers a body in a locked room of the Colorado castle, transforming everyone in Vanessa's family into potential killers.

Prologue

The tears leaked out of Kay Duvall's eyes, even as she tried to
focus on what she had to do. *Had* to do to bring Ben home safe.

She fumbled with her ID and punched in the code that
would open the side door, usually only used for a guard taking a
smoke break. It would be easy for the men behind her to escape
from this side of the prison.

It went against everything she was supposed to do.
Everything she considered right and good.

A quiet sob escaped her lips. They had her son. How could
she not help them escape? Nothing mattered beyond her son's
life.

"Would you stop already?" one of the prisoners muttered.
He'd made her give him her gun, which he now jabbed into her
back. "Crying isn't going to change anything. So just shut up."

She didn't care so much about her own life or if she'd be
fired. She didn't care what happened to her as long as they let
her son go. So she swallowed down the sobs and blinked out as
many tears as she could, hoping to stem the tide of them.

She got the door open and slid out first—because the man holding the gun pushed it into her back until she moved forward.

They came through the door behind her, dressed in the clothes she'd stolen from the locker room and Lost and Found. Anything warm she could get her hands on to help them escape into the frigid February night.

Help them escape. Help three dangerous men escape prison. When she was supposed to keep them inside.

It didn't matter anymore. She just wanted them gone. If they were gone, they'd let her baby go. They had to let her baby go.

Kay forced her legs to move, one foot in front of the other, toward the gate she could unlock without setting off any alarms. She unlocked it, steadier this time if only because she kept thinking that once they were gone, she could get in contact with Ben.

She flung open the gate and gestured them out into the parking lot. "Stay out of the safety lights and no one should bug you."

"You better hope not," one of the men growled.

"The minute you sound that alarm, your kid is dead. You got it?" This one was the ringleader. The one who'd been in for murder. Who else would he kill out there in the world?

Guilt pooled in Kay's belly, but she had to ignore it. She had to live with it. Whatever guilt she felt would be survivable. Living without her son wouldn't be. Besides, she had to believe they'd be caught. They'd do something else terrible and be caught.

As long as her son was alive, she didn't care.

Don't miss
Hunting a Killer *by Nicole Helm,*
available February 2021 wherever
Harlequin Intrigue books and ebooks are sold.

Harlequin.com

HIEXP0121